# *Astronomical Odds*

## Third Flatiron Anthologies
## Volume 3, Spring 2014

### Edited by Juliana Rew
### Cover Art by Keely Rew

# Dedication

For all of us who felt the odds were stacked against us but managed to beat them somehow.

# Astronomical Odds
## Third Flatiron Anthologies
## Volume 3, Spring 2014

Published by Third Flatiron Publishing
Juliana Rew, Editor

**Discover other titles by Third Flatiron:**
(1) Over the Brink: Tales of Environmental Disaster

(2) A High Shrill Thump: War Stories

(3) Origins: Colliding Causalities

(4) Universe Horribilis

(5) Playing with Fire

(6) Lost Worlds, Retraced

(7) Redshifted: Martian Stories

# Contents

\*\*\*\*\*~~~~~\*\*\*\*\*

# In the Blood

### by Ken Altabef

Brother Dill's Traveling Circus and Roadside Carnival passed through Carson City in October 1882. We've played a lot of towns and dragged a lot of country miles, but I'll never forget that one, no sir.

Autumn rain had turned the dirt roads to red mud as we pulled in, as wet and bedraggled a troupe as you ever did see. While the main company pounded stakes, the sideshow barkers went to work drumming up business. I set to putting up our little stage, my son Matthew holding the boards in place while I screwed them in. Then I stood him atop his soapbox.

"You okay?" I asked.

"Fine, Pa," he answered. That was my boy, always short on words. Ten years old, he was a quiet one. Maybe life on the road's not much good for a boy, I don't know. He seemed half scared to death most of the time, though he wouldn't speak of it, and looked at people fair strange when they weren't looking back. But a very good boy. And that was the day I'll always remember, the day everything changed.

I wiped the slick drizzle from my forehead, pulled on a soggy old top hat, and warmed up my ten-dollar words.

"Ladies and gen'lemen! Gather 'round. Gather 'round," I hollered. "Here to amaze, here to astound your sensibilities, I present to you my son Matthew, the Amazin' Matthew, the Boy Genius!"

We gathered a fair crowd of about twenty curiosity seekers around, and the rain finally stopped.

"My son, this fine young man you see here before you," I pitched, "whose brain is an amazin' calculatin'

7

machine. Let me have two numbers, gen'lemen, the biggest you can think of."

"Twenty-six!" threw out one bedraggled soul.

"Fifty-seven!" added another.

"All right, all right. We have twenty-six and fifty-seven, and this little lad here will multiply these two numbers against themselves on the instant."

I brought my arm around in a grand, sweeping arc that ended at the soapbox. "The answer, Matthew?"

"One thousan' four hunnert an' eighty-two," he said calmly.

"There you have it, folks. The Boy Genius. Have you ever before witnessed such a thing?"

This statement was met with the usual disarray among the crowd. None of them knew if the answer was correct. Someone came up with the bright idea to call in the town assayer. They acted as if they expected me to object, but I went and cheered them on.

"A fine idea," I said, "Go an' get him!"

My biggest problem was holding the crowd until this assayer fellow showed up. To that end I launched into a couple of bawdy jokes, real crowd-pleasers such as the one about the doctor and the milkmaid.

After a few, the assayer appeared through the gathering crowd. A tall man in pinstripe jacket and cornsack pants, he looked the educated type. He even wore gold-rimmed spectacles.

"What was the question?" he asked in a pale, reedy voice.

"Twenty-six times by fifty-seven," I said.

All eyes turned to the assayer. The accountant withdrew paper and pencil and began figuring the answer. It took a few minutes. Usually the longer it takes the better for me in the end. The crowd was just getting restless, when he barked out: "1,482!"

I threw both arms toward Matthew and boomed, "Correct! Boy Genius has done it again! Have you ever seen the like?" A mixed response from the crowd. This was maybe taking a bit too long. "Care to give it another try?" I said. "Any two numbers. . . "

"Seventeen," suggested a portly rancher.

"And the other?"

The assayer said, "One thousand fifty three."

I put on a worried look and exhaled mightily. I dry-washed my face with my hands. "All right then," I said in a shaky voice. "Seventeen taken by one thousan' an' fifty-three."

My boy hesitated not a bit. "Seventeen thousan' nine hunnert an' one."

"Aha!" I said. "If I was a bettin' man. . . "

"Ten dollars!" said one cowpoke.

"Twenty!"

"But no, no," I added, "That wouldn't be fair. This is a boy genius here. I wouldn't want to take advantage."

Laughs from the crowd. All eyes turned toward the assayer as he began figuring madly.

"I'm sorry," he said at last, "But the boy is wrong. I get one thousand one hundred and six."

A chorus of boos and hisses rose up. The crowd jostled, threatening to break apart.

"Now wait one minute!" I said. "You there!" I pointed toward the assayer. "Well sir, I suggest you check your 'rithmatic again. You see, my boy is never wrong. Never!"

The crowd drifted back as the assayer took up his pencil again. In the end he doffed his porkpie hat, made a comical little bow, and said. "My apologies, good people. The sum is indeed 17,901. The boy is correct!"

A tremendous cheer rang out.

"Incredible! Incredible!" I purred. As I set out my top hat to catch their jubilant donations, a well-dressed man delivered a note on fine paper. Of course I couldn't read it, but I called Matthew to my side. He piped up: "Arthur Doakes and son, you are cordially invited to

9

partake dinner at the home of Mr. W. Calhoun at six o'clock this evening."

William Donner Calhoun, head honcho of the Virginia and Truckee Railroad, was the richest man in town.

"See, boy?" I said. "We're finally comin' up in the world."

...

The same manservant who had passed me the note at the carnival let us in. I'm afraid Matthew and I looked a sad sight, as we were still damp and the long walk up the hill to Calhoun's had left us tracking mud. The butler insisted we take off our boots and ran to get us each a fresh pair of socks.

Calhoun's study was a large rectangular room dressed up like the inside of a railway car with fine mahogany panels along the walls and a doorway at either end. The wall behind his desk was lined with bookshelves holding all sorts of odd and sundry items. Children's wind-up toys, music boxes, a balsa wood model of a frigate, and a couple of animal skulls, too. I guess rich people collect anything they want. One skull came from some sort of a gorilla. The other was even uglier. It was the skull of a cat, a real big one by the looks, with eye teeth long as knives. It seemed like something Brother Dill would have put in his freak show to chill the spines of his hapless marks, but I guess those huge fangs weren't glued on. Somehow I don't think Mr. Calhoun would take much truck with fakes.

Calhoun strode into the room. A tall man, clean-shaved with sandy hair cut neat. He wore a sleek blue jacket of the military style trimmed with gold at the cuffs and collar.

He extended his hand. "Mr. Doakes."

I returned a firm grip, saying, "A pleasure, sir."

Calhoun nodded at Matthew. "A fine-looking boy. Mrs. Heller informs me dinner will be ready shortly."

Just the mention started my stomach to rumbling. "What, sir, exactly will we be havin'?" Calhoun chuckled. "Roast turkey, sweet potatoes, string beans. Rum cake."

I nearly fell over.

"Can I offer you a brandy before dinner?" he asked.

"Don't mind if I do."

He took a crystal decanter from his desk. "Your boy has an amazing mind. That's quite a trick he does."

"No trick, sir," I said. "He's a calculatin' machine. Any two numbers. . . "

"Any two?" asked Calhoun. "What if I say fifty-seven?"

"Right as rain," I said. "And the other?"

Calhoun turned to Matthew. "You pick one."

The boy blinked uncertainly.

"Well go ahead," I said. "Don't be rude."

"Seventy-eight," Matthew said meekly.

"Okay," agreed Calhoun. "Fifty-seven times seventy-eight, and that makes. . . "

"Four thousan' four hunnert forty-six," said Matthew. But the thing of it was—Calhoun recited the number at the exact same time. Now I really did go weak at the knees.

"Yes," said Calhoun, "I can do it too. Your boy does not calculate the numbers, Mr. Doakes. He has instead a terrific memory. He's memorized the multiplication tables as far as the eye can see. So it is, in fact, a trick."

"And you can do it too?"

"Yes. Having a memory for figures is quite an asset for an engineer. That's how I got to the top of the rail business. That, and a lot of hard work, mind you. But a memory for figures and detail, yes, and a memory for what people say, for their different facial expressions. I don't suggest you try to lie to me Mr. Doakes. I'll know it just by your face."

11

"No sir."

"I remember everything," said Calhoun. "I recall the day I came screaming into this world. I remember my circumcision, the sting of the doctor's knife, five days old. My first birthday too. I remember all of it, every detail."

Calhoun looked at me with such a mix of pain and pleasure in his eyes I didn't doubt a word of it. He went on, "But having a terrific memory has its drawbacks too. I remember all sorts of things. I remember people, places, things that happened in the past. I pass a man on the street and I remember he was my frigate Captain, a hundred and fifty-years ago. I look at my friend, Bill Johnston, and I remember that same man as a French Lieutenant on the fields of Gananoque. He died in my arms in 1812. But Bill Johnston, he doesn't remember any of it at all."

Calhoun spoke to Matthew as much as to me, and damn if he wasn't studying that boy's face.

"I run into people all the time, but they don't remember the things I remember. I walk among them, a stranger drowning in a sea of familiar faces. This type of thing wears on a man, Mr. Doakes. Sometimes a body gets to thinking he might be crazy, living like that."

Calhoun gave my son a look I didn't very much care for. I was just on the point of protest, when I noticed Matthew's reaction. I took a fortifying sip of brandy.

"And so I ask," said Calhoun, "What do you remember, boy?"

"I. . . " said Matthew hesitantly. He walked over to the curio shelf. He indicated the gigantic cat skull with the dagger-teeth. "I remember that."

"That's very old," said Calhoun. "My friends in New York call it a sabre-tooth tiger. And just what do you remember about that?"

"I remember the smell of its blood."

"Matthew!"

"No, it's all right," insisted Calhoun. "Let the boy speak."

## In the Blood

"I remember that it was death. . . sudden death for any of our people, 'nless we were very careful. We hunted that thing. But we had. . . we had to do it smart-like. I made the noises to scare it. 'Aroo, aroo' I would say, while the others, they went sneakin' aroun' the other way. And I remember my heart beatin' fast, so fast because that thing was death. But if you got it lined up jus' right in the canyon. . . "

"Yes, that's right," added Calhoun. "If we kept its back to the rocks it would get skittish. And again, if a few of us came at it to one side, it would run the other way."

My boy Matthew nodded, saying, "An' then someone would take his spear an' neck it. I remember the taste. The salt an' the fire. An' the blood."

"Yes," Calhoun said. "Its blood was sweet."

Then Matthew and Mr. Calhoun both together, cried out, "Hurrragghh!"

I can't describe the unearthly chill it caused me to hear that guttural sound coming from my son's lips.

Calhoun straightened his coat, momentarily embarrassed. He chuckled. "Indeed I believe I just heard the dinner bell tolling."

He put his arm around Matthew's shoulder and offered me a friendly nod. "Only one way to settle my mind, but what were the chances of finding another like me? Let's head into dinner. We've quite a lot to talk about."

And that night my quiet little boy talked and talked and talked.

###

## About the Author

New York writer Ken Altabef's short fiction has appeared three times in *The Magazine of Fantasy & Science Fiction* as well as *Interzone, Abyss & Apex,*

*Buzzymag, Stupefying Stories, Unsettling Wonder*, and various anthologies.

*Way of the Shaman*, his 5-part series of epic fantasy novels, is published by Blueberry Lane Books. You can preview this work and others at the author website, www.wayoftheshamanONLINE.com

\*\*\*\*\*~~~\*\*\*\*\*

# Garden of Fog and Monsters

by Michelle Ann King

I wake up stretched out flat on the floor, one arm trapped underneath me and a dry, sour taste in my mouth. I roll over, wait out the pain that fizzes in my fingers as the circulation returns, then haul myself to my feet.

In the stories I read as a kid, this sort of thing was easy—people flew into a wormhole, or stepped into a transporter beam, or just clicked their ruby red shoes together and wished really hard. There was no fuss, no pain, and certainly no vomiting.

These stories ended up being wrong about most things, so I don't know why I expected this to be any different.

The room I've arrived in is green, featureless, and about four metres square. I'm alone.

Alone. I know the word, but the experience is a new one. I don't think I've ever been in an empty building in my life. There's just no such thing, back on poor old choked, overpopulated Earth.

It's a strange sensation, and I'm not sure I like it. I feel a bit like I've lost a limb.

The only item in the room is a single All-In pushed up against the back wall. No, not an All-In. A cot. It's just a frame and mattress; no storage, no electronics, no other function. Furniture, not equipment. Shockingly wasteful. At home, anything that takes up space has to earn its keep. But then this isn't home, is it? And lack of space isn't the problem out here.

The official name for this place is the Interstice, but everybody I know calls it the Garden of Eden. A world of primordial soup—or primordial fog, to be exact—just waiting to be moulded and shaped into your personal version of paradise.

15

They created a whole new branch of physics to make sense of it, but everybody was way more interested in the practical applications than the theorems. Rolling green hills and crystal blue lakes? You got it. A skyscraper fifteen miles high? You got it. Furry purple dinosaurs? You got it. In this garden, everybody's God.

I run my hand over the wall. It looks metallic but feels soft to the touch and slightly clammy, as if not quite cooked. I wipe my hand on my trousers and sit on the cot. They told me the facilities would be basic, and they weren't joking. But it makes sense. There's no point going to a lot of trouble over a place like this. It's a holding pen, that's all.

For the first time, I notice there's no door. Suppose that makes sense, too.

"Hello, Irene," a voice says.

It sounds like someone whispering in both ears at once, and it makes me jump. They told me about this, too—again, no point sending anyone in person—but it's another strange sensation. I don't like it any better than the first one.

"I'm sorry," the voice goes on, "I didn't mean to startle you. I'm Conrad, one of the administrators here. Is there anything you need?"

I rub my arms, bare in the military-issue singlet. It's cold in here. "No. Just point me at the ring, the arena, whatever."

My sister went nuts when I told her I'd signed up for this. But she's having twins, for the love of God. What other option have we got? You can't bring up a baby—two babies—where we are. We share a squat with twenty others at any given time, and everybody's practically sleeping on top of each other as it is. And that's when they're not trying to rob or kill each other. Petra's kids will never know their father, because he got shot over a cache of illegal implants before she even knew she was pregnant. We can't go on like that.

## Garden of Fog and Monsters

They used to have nurseries, in the old days. I read about it. A whole room, just for a baby. They used to have gardens, parks, places for kids to play. We could have all that, in the Garden of Eden.

If we're allowed through the gates, of course.

The official line is that after negotiations with the inhabitants, an agreement was reached to accommodate settlers. Which most people take to mean that we tried to wipe them out and take it for ourselves, but got our arses kicked.

Plenty of people—not just Petra—call the agreement barbaric. But if you ask me, it's fair enough. The aliens were here first, so they get to set the price of admission. Their territory, their rules. If they want to set up a fight to the death, the old "two enter, one leaves" routine, it's up to them. And people can act as horrified as they like, but it's not as if that's a new—or alien, ha ha—concept to us, is it?

"Would you like to rest first?" Conrad says. "I know the transition can be debilitating."

His voice is low, a little fuzzy. I don't know how they do broadcast out here—there's nothing in this room that looks like a comm system, or tech of any sort—but it doesn't matter. They did try to tell me about some of those new laws of physics in my briefing, but I didn't pay much attention. Like a wise man once said, if it takes fifty pages of mathematical equations to explain, you might as well call it magic and be done with it.

"No. I'm fine. Just tell me one thing, Conrad. My sister gets her relocation because I'm taking part, right? It doesn't matter whether I win or lose the actual fight."

"That's correct," he says.

"Good. Then let's get on with it."

"Are you sure? I could provide you with water, or something to eat, or—"

I laugh. "Is this the training montage part of the show? Do you teach me to handle alien weapons and learn

17

special moves? To meditate, ground myself, and find my secret inner strength? Do you tell me how to beat them?"

There's a pause, then he says, "No."

"No. I didn't think so." I laugh again. "Don't worry about it, Conrad. I know what I signed up for. I've got no illusions."

They pitch it to you as a contest, back home. A test of strength and skill. Something you've got a chance to win.

And sure, there are plenty who believe it. They're always broadcasting confident interviews with the volunteers beforehand, and glowing reports about their wonderful new lives afterward. But I know my history, and the gladiators always killed the slaves. The lions always ate the Christians. And while you get to see the families in the Interstice, posing in front of their fabulous mansions or castles or whatever, you know who you don't see? The volunteers themselves. You don't see them. In fact, you never see them again.

"Come on," I say. "Open up and let me out of this place. I'm getting claustrophobic."

"Are you—"

I hold up my hands. "For the love of whatever passes for God out here, can we please just get this over with?"

He doesn't argue any more. The green surface in front of me shimmers and transforms into a transparent silvery grey. I reach out, and my hand passes through. There's a suggestion of shape, of slowly swirling movement, but nothing that the eye can keep in focus. It's hypnotising and nauseating in equal measure. I step through the green walls, and they're swallowed up behind me.

"So this is it? I thought paradise was supposed to come with palm trees, huh?" I shake my head. "Nothing ever lives up to the advertising, does it?"

"This area is undeveloped," Conrad says. "Raw material. We have to construct our paradise out of it."

And with that, a pair of palm trees with a bright red hammock slung between them comes looming out of the fog. He's got a sense of humour, this guy, you've got to give him points for that.

I crouch down, pick up a handful of silky, warm sand, and try not to look impressed. "Magic," I whisper.

I stand up, and the trees fade back into the mist. From behind them, something else detaches itself. It's huge and oddly shaped, but that's all I can tell. I can't make out any detail. Which is probably for the best.

My legs are trembling, the thigh muscles threatening to go into spasm. It's so cold out here. The indistinct shape drifts closer. Something glows red in the fog. Are they eyes?

I wrap my arms around myself. "Is this it, then? Is it happening? Right now?"

"Yes."

I nod. "Okay. Okay."

He doesn't respond. All I can hear is breathing. It's not my own.

"Conrad? Are you there?"

"I'm here, Irene."

"Has anyone ever killed one of them? Tell me the truth. All the people who came out here. Did any of them ever win?" I don't even know why I'm asking. I don't have a weapon, and never expected to be offered one.

"No," Conrad says.

An honest lad, too. More points.

The shape in the fog is close, now. Close enough for me to realise that it's not so much a being, a creature, at all—more a collection of sensations and half-formed thoughts.

A blood vessel in my eye must have burst, because my vision is swimming with red. I blink hard and hot, gritty tears squeeze out. They feel like acid on my cheeks. "Tell my sister I love her."

"You'll be able to tell her yourself," he says.

I try to say that I don't understand, but my mouth won't form the words. The cold—or maybe the fog—is so heavy, so clinging. Pressing down. Draining my strength.

"You will," he says, and I can no longer tell whether the voice is coming from the facility behind me, from inside my head, or from the thing looming above me.

"You can't tell, because there's no difference, Irene."

My legs give way and tip me onto the ground. It's firm, even though I can't see it through the fog.

"They can't be killed," Conrad's voice goes on. "They're not alive, not in the sense that humans understand it. They're part of the Interstice itself, and that cannot be destroyed any more than raw energy can. So all those rumours about the war were correct: the humans had their arses comprehensively kicked." He sounds amused.

I try to swallow, but there's no saliva in my mouth. My voice comes out as a croak, barely recognisable. I am so cold. "So this is, what? Revenge? Payback?"

"No, no. Nothing like that. This is healing."

I want to say *I don't understand* again, but I think I'm starting to. I close my eyes, and the fog still swirls behind my eyelids.

"The closest we can get is to say they're a hive mind. A combined sentience. Humans were a shock to them. The individuality, the separateness. It's abhorrent, an open wound. They want to fix it, restore the broken part to the whole. It's why the volunteers are all people like you, Irene. People who understand family, connection, love. It makes you—"

"What? Easier to digest?"

"We prefer the word incorporate."

I shake my head, but I can't clear the fog out of it. I hold up my hand, and the flesh looks grey. Misty. Like it's coming apart.

"It's all right," Conrad says. I can feel him smile. I don't know how, but I can. "It only hurts for a little while."

Of course. I get it now. Should have seen it before. Conrad was a volunteer.

"Yes," he says.

My head is too heavy to hold up any more, and I let it hang down. The fog supports me. I suppose it figures—there's always a price to pay for power. For wishes that come true. Maybe the old stories knew something after all.

I can feel my heartbeat slowing, my bones melting, my blood drying up and blowing away.

I look around—I can see so widely now, so clearly—and the alien is waiting there to catch me.

But he doesn't look so alien any more.

"You were right," I say, although I know it isn't really speaking. Hasn't been for a while. "It doesn't hurt for long."

He smiles. We all do.

And I see that I was right about something, too. This is a good place for a newborn.

### 

### About the Author

Michelle Ann King writes science fiction, fantasy, and horror from her kitchen table in Essex, England. Her stories have appeared in various venues, including *Daily Science Fiction, Penumbra Magazine,* and *Drabblecast.* She loves Las Vegas, zombie films, and good Scotch whisky. Find details of her books and stories at www.transientcactus.co.uk

*****~~~~~*****

# From Here to the Northern Line

by Edoardo Albert

"Mr. Mannion?"

"Yes?" I rubbed the sleep from my eyes and peered blearily at the two uniformed men standing at the door.

"Transport Police. We're here to interview your son."

"Huh?"

"Your son," explained the more grizzled-looking of the pair. "We want to talk to him."

The mention of police had, I thought, banished sleep completely. "I beg your pardon," I said, attempting the hauteur of Lady Bracknell and achieving the foppishness of Algernon Moncrieff.

"There is a serious matter concerning your son. We need to talk to him. Now."

I shook my head. This did not make sense. "Hang on a minute. We are talking about the same boy here? Graeme? Graeme Mannion? The sort of boy who tells me to slow down when I'm doing 31 miles per hour in a 30 miles-per-hour zone. The boy who got voted least likely to get in trouble with the police five years running at his school. You want to speak to him?"

"Yes," said the younger policeman. "We want to see Graeme Mannion."

"Well, I'm afraid you're out of luck. He's out." I began to close the door, but the older officer put his hand against it. The door stopped dead, as if it had run into a wall. I pushed harder, but it was like shoving concrete.

"Where is he?" asked the younger officer.

"I don't know. Out."

"You allow your young son to wander about without any idea of where he's gone or when he'll be

23

back?" The policeman raised an eyebrow. I was beginning to dislike him. "I wonder what the social services would say about this?" he said, turning to his colleague.

The older policeman tsked loudly. "Not very good parenting."

Then they both turned and stared at me.

I said, "You do know he's 17?"

There was silence. The older policeman said, "I knew that."

"Me too," said the younger one.

"Being 17—as you say you knew—you'll understand that my son could be back at any time. So I suggest you come back later." I began to shut the door. But the older policeman got his hand in the gap as the door closed. Well, 'squelched' might be a more accurate description of what happened.

"Ow," said the older policeman.

I looked at the fingers caught in the door jam, and was impressed that he'd been able to say anything at all.

"That must have hurt." I pulled the door open.

The policeman wrung out his hand, but other than that he seemed remarkably unbothered that his fingers had been crushed. "It did." He wrapped a white handkerchief around his fingers, and, without looking up, said to his partner, "Officer Black, please serve Mr. Mannion with the warrant."

An unimpeachably legal-looking document was held before my eyes, apparently giving them the right to enter my home, take it apart, remove whatever they wanted, and, who knows, sleep with my wife. Since we were a court case away from the divorce becoming final, they were welcome to her, but I wasn't too happy about the rest of it.

"Are you going to let us pass, or do we have to force our way in?" asked Officer Black.

"Which would you prefer?"

"Do you have to ask?" The young policeman cracked his knuckles. Despite the situation, I could hardly stop myself giggling. It was like having two bad actors on my doorstep. I half expected to see a director standing somewhere out of shot.

"Be my guest." I stepped back.

The policemen filed in.

"Graeme's room's upstairs. Straight ahead of you."

I followed them half way up the stairs and then stopped. The two men were standing on either side of the closed door to Graeme's room, backs to the wall, guns drawn.

Guns drawn?

"What—" I began, but then discovered that having someone point a gun at me is an efficient method of shutting me up. Officer Black held his finger to his lips.

I wanted to tell him that Graeme really wasn't in there, but, well, he was pointing a gun at me.

"One, two, three." The men mouthed the words, and then they went in, the older policeman forcing the door back and sweeping his revolver around in a broad, two-handed arc, while the younger and more athletic Officer Black rolled in to the room, his gun sweeping the far corners.

I wanted to applaud. I settled for pointing out that I'd told them Graeme wasn't in.

"Where is he, then?" asked Officer Black, shouldering his pistol.

"Out. With his mother."

"At this time?"

"He stayed with her yesterday. We're not together any more." I looked at the alarm clock. "He said something about going to watch some trains this morning and then going to school."

"Why didn't you take him to see the train?" asked the older policeman.

25

I looked at him incredulously. "Would you want to get up at some godforsaken hour in the morning to stand on a windy platform and watch trains rattling by?"

The older policeman thought about it for a while. "Yes," he said.

"We are the Transport Police," added Officer Black.

I was being warranted by the league of trainspotters.

"Transport Police. Naturally you like trains. Professional interest, I suppose."

But the police were no longer interested in conversation.

"Officer White, take a look at this." The young Officer Black pointed at Graeme's desk. "What do you think?"

They hunched over the desk. I sidled closer to see what they were poring over and remained mystified at their interest. They were pointing at, and whispering over, Graeme's railway and tube maps. He draws them himself, obsessively copying out the different routes. If I ever needed to get anywhere, all I had to do was ask Graeme, and he'd reel off the answer, complete with alternative routes should there be delays on any of the lines. Graeme's got Asperger's Syndrome, and trains are his thing. They have been ever since he was two; he and I spent many a cold, windy Saturday morning on railway platforms watching trains while his mother got a lie in. At least, that's what she'd told me at the time.

I could see them pointing from one map to another, whispering back and forth as if Graeme had copied down state secrets.

"Come on," I said, "it's not against the law to draw the tube map."

Officers White and Black turned round. They were each holding one of Graeme's maps in the corner-of-the-paper fashion of a policeman handling vital evidence.

"Copyright."

I looked from one man to the other and back again. Neither cracked a smile.

"Come on. You're not trying to tell me it's against the law for a boy to copy out the tube map?"

Officer White and Officer Black stared at me. They still weren't smiling.

"This is a very serious matter," began Officer Black.

"Intellectual property rights are the basis of all modern civilizations," continued Officer White.

"And your son is flagrantly violating them," they finished in unison.

Up until that day, I could have counted the occasions I'd been lost for words on my thumbs. The day's events were calling in my fingers.

"We'll be taking all this in as evidence," said Officer White, as Officer Black carefully placed Graeme's painstakingly drawn maps on top of each other.

"Bag them, Officer Black."

Officer Black stopped what he was doing.

"Why do I always have to do the bagging?"

"Because you have the bags."

"Oh. Right." Officer Black began putting the maps into clear plastic folders that seemed to shrink to fit as they were placed on.

"You've got self-laminating bags," I said.

"Oh, yes, these," said Officer Black, looking at the bag in his hand as if he was seeing it for the first time. "Why do I always carry the bags?"

"Because you have pockets," said Officer White.

"Oh. Right." Officer Black went back to bagging. Officer White was going through the other things on Graeme's desk. Neither of them was paying any attention to me. So I toed Graeme's latest, incomplete map under the bed. I didn't see why they should get all of Graeme's work. He'd spend hours, days sometimes, working on his maps. It was just a shame all he did was copy. There was a time when I thought Graeme would grow up to be a great painter, but I guess my originality gene didn't get through.

"Is that everything, Officer Black?"

"That's everything, Officer White."

The Transport Police, packed and bagged, turned to go.

"Don't I get a receipt?" I asked, innocently enough. It was thus thoroughly satisfying to see the glances bouncing back and forth, and whispers, "I thought you wrote one" and "I thought you did" and "How was I supposed to write a receipt *and* bag up all the evidence?"

Officer White's smile, when he turned it on me, was significantly less dazzling than before.

"One moment, please." He got out a pad and started scribbling furiously. Officer Black, meanwhile, was finding the corners of the room most interesting.

"Nice weather," he said, when he accidentally caught my eye.

I thought back over the last few weeks of unseasonable cold, rain, and wind.

"No."

"I meant, it's nice to have some weather."

"As opposed to not having any weather?"

"Er, yes." Officer Black cast a glance in the direction of his partner. "Are you finished yet, Officer White?"

"Here." Officer White tore off the top sheet of paper and handed it to me. "Now, we must be off. . ."

"You haven't signed it."

"What?"

I pointed. "You haven't signed it."

Officer White snatched the receipt, scrawled an illegible signature, and handed it back.

"There. Let's go, Officer Black."

"With you there, Officer White."

I followed the men to the door and watched them march to their car. Once they were safely out of the way, I went back upstairs and retrieved the map. For policemen, they didn't seem much good at searches. But there was always the chance they'd come back, and it was too much to hope they'd miss it a second time, so I needed to find somewhere safer to hide it.

It really was a beautiful piece of work. It was only a pity that Graeme didn't lavish the same attention on his school work. The way he drew the line from Edgware to. . . I shook my head and retraced the route. That was odd. The Northern Line didn't go there, did it? What on earth was Graeme drawing?

I began to smile. Maybe the boy was actually developing an imagination.

...

Graeme came in, sat down at the table, and began taking his notebook, camera, and flask from his backpack and arranging them on the table—and yes, my teenage son really does carry around a thermos flask of tea. He placed the camera in front of him, so he could review the photos; the notebook, on his right, so he could label the photos correctly; and the flask, to his left, ready to be washed out. He didn't say, "Hello," but then, he usually doesn't unless reminded.

"Hello," I said.

"Hello, Dad." Graeme didn't look up from what he was doing.

"Some people called to see you."

Graeme didn't answer. He was staring at the camera display, his nose wrinkled, eyes squinting and mouth scrunched. It was a characteristic expression. It meant something did not compute.

"The Transport Police. They took away your maps. All except this one." I laid Graeme's latest effort on the table, moving the camera to make room.

We stared down at a map that, although ostensibly a normal diagram of the London Underground, had all sorts of additional lines, stations, and termini.

"I didn't know the other branch of the Northern Line terminated at Clarke Skyhook. The line from Betelgeuse E to Zenobia, via Place de la Concord is a new one to me too."

Graeme looked up with the sort of embarrassed smile that meant he was about to lie, excruciatingly badly.

I held up my hand. "Don't say it."

"But. . . "

"Don't say that either."

"But. . . "

"Shh." I put a finger to my lips. "Now, what did we learn in Psych classes? It's all right to make things up, Graeme. It's called imagination. It's fun, not lying."

"But. . . "

"That's three buts, Graeme." I patted his head. "I don't feel any horns." I looked closely at his temples. "I don't see any horns. Therefore, you are not a goat, so don't go butting me, right. Now, why are the Transport Police looking for you? I can't believe you've been fare dodging or doing anything wrong, God forbid." I crossed myself in an old, half-remembered gesture, mainly because it would annoy Graeme, who hated casual blasphemy.

I suppose I must have been more upset by the raid than I'd realised.

"But, Dad, that's what I've been trying to tell you," wailed Graeme. "It's true. It's not made up."

"Oh, come on. You'll be telling me you've been to—" I glanced at the map and pointed at an unlikely sounding station, "Willesden Junction next."

"Yes," said Graeme. "So've you. When we went to see the trains on the West Coast Main Line from Euston."

"Oh, that occasion of joy. Well, I might have been *there*, but what about this station?"

"Trantor," read out Graeme, peering over my finger. "It's a bit busy. I didn't stay long."

"Oh, come on, Graeme. You're not telling me you've been to all these places: La Defence, Riga 3, Bowling Green; you're making them up."

Graeme looked puzzled. Not that that was unusual: he almost always looked puzzled. It was bloody annoying.

"They take the Oyster card, Dad. I didn't cheat."

"There's less chance of you cheating than. . . than of me getting back with your mum. Come on, though, these are just stations you've read about, right?"

Graeme looked thoughtful. "If I cheated on something, would you get back with Mum?"

"No! Now answer the question."

"It might be better if I showed you, Dad," said Graeme.

Which was how I wound up on a platform staring up at the star formations of the Lesser Magellanic Cloud while listening for announcements on the late running train to the Milky Way.

Turns out, you can get anywhere on the tube. Who'd have known?

Graeme, that's who. Being Asperger's and obsessed with detail, he'd spotted the modified tube maps and unmarked interchanges that put passengers onto the galactic transport network, and explored them.

"So," I said, trying to sound insouciant as two large carnids walked past, "why are the Transport Police after you?"

"I don't think we're supposed to know about the tube. Lots of aliens use Earth as a dormitory planet—it's very convenient for the Spiral Arms—and prices would rocket if the news got out at home."

"Really?"

...

Six months later, 17 galactic realtors and 34 surveyors had set up offices on Earth, people were

31

holidaying in the Milky Way and commuting to Andromeda, I was a very, very, very rich man, and Graeme was the most famous train spotter in history.

Thermos flasks were most definitely in.

### 

## About the Author

Edoardo Albert is, on paper at least, a surprisingly exotic creature: Italian, Sinhala, and Tamil by background, he grew up in London among the polyglot children of immigrants (it was only when he went to university that he actually got to know any English people). He avers that he once reduced a reader to helpless, hysterical laughter. Unfortunately, the piece that did so was a lonely-hearts ad. The first volume of his trilogy on the Dark-Age kings of Britain, The Northumbrian Thrones, is out next March from Lion Fiction, titled Edwin: High King of Britain. He lives online at www.edoardoalbert.com, on Twitter @EdoardoAlbert, and Facebook too.

*****~~~~~*****

# Mother of All

by John A. McColley

Pala Ai sat in the deep dark of her chamber. Servants moved about, taking newly lain eggs to incubation chambers, bringing her food. She was the latest of a thousand Queens, and each of their memories were hers. They helped her rule twenty million subjects. Someday, she would have many times that, her empire grown through satellite colonies watched over by her daughters. Each, she would take to the Common Place, where scent messages and tactile communication were unnecessary. Here, minds mingled, and information flowed with the speed of thought.

The final day of her own training was still strong in her recollection. Most memories bled together. Only their essences, the salient aspect of events, resolutions remained, the easier to store, to pass on. That day washed over her now. . . She had flown for the last time, toward the sun, then south, following a stream to a place where plants grew tall, signifying rich soil and few rocks. Before breaking ground, she had surveyed the land, the nearby water sources, vegetation. She referred to that mental map every day as she directed workers to excavate tunnels and chambers.

She dug straight down, an antenna length, a body length before backing out. The last clump of earth still between her mandibles, she walked around the opening leaving scent markings meaning "home" and "dig." When she came back to the spot where she'd started her circuit, she sat, settling into the Common Place. Sensing the many around her, she directed those few hundred drones and workers. They dug quickly, creating the first chamber eight body lengths down, the second at twelve. She descended into the lower chamber, resting while the others completed the map of the first, tiny colony she had implanted in their minds. It was the last day she had seen the sun for herself.

...

The colony bloomed down and down, spreading from the main stem of that tunnel she'd bored herself, leading, strong. They dug incubation chambers, mold farms, rearing rooms for first instars, second instars. Hundreds became thousands became millions.

Only she had a name, and only she knew it. Only she had a sense of self beyond the colony, though, of course, only she was integral to it. Workers needed not trouble themselves with intellect beyond following her commands to collect this or dig that. They moved through life in their tiny little consciousnesses, never knowing the fullness of the Common Place. This place was hers alone, a mental state in which she could monitor the goings-on in the colony, observe through others' senses, send commands.

The Common Place was her trade-off for being immobile. She gave up her legs, as her abdomen grew into an egg producing machine, distended, heavier itself than her whole body before, trapping her in the royal chamber. Her mind was free to wander, though, observing tunnels and even the surface around all the entrances of the colony through the eyes of others. It was important to keep an updated map, but she also enjoyed it, seeing the wind riffle the leaves and grasses, hearing the stream nearby sing over waterfalls and stones.

Pala Ai sat, ovulating, always ovulating, in the Common Place, taking stock of food reserves, the state of the mold farms, the progress on new tunnels and chambers. She calculated the number of workers, drones, various instars down to eggs and their needs to determine how much more food they would need before the cold came and how close they would get to that quota with everyone doing as they were. Probabilities were high. She did not like probabilities, being steeped in the certainty of the past, but they were her responsibility. The Queen's purpose was not only to provide the next generation, but to ensure it was provided for.

Her workers were busy, and she was busy keeping them on the right task at the right time. Alarm registered in one scout who stood atop a rock a few hundred body lengths from the main entrance. The sun shone bright on the broad plain around the hive. Workers trekked out north and west in search of fodder for the mold farms. The clouds were high and thin. It had not rained in some time. The air was dry, the nearby stream a mere trickle.

The sun stood to the east, midway between the horizon and the apex. Another light grew some degrees above. It began as a sliding point, a quickly moving star, but in moments it had grown to half the size of the blue sun. Intrigued, Queen Pala Ai kept the worker's eyes trained on the spectacle. Of all the things she had seen and imagined in her deep, safe laying chamber, this was the most stunning. A second sun! How did this bode for the rain which had been so scarce? Was it a sign from the sky that the drought was over, or a threat of worse to come? Nothing in her personal memories or those left over from her ancestors revealed the answer. This in itself was troubling, but exciting.

The blazing star grew, leaving a trail of incandescent smoke that turned black as though it punctured the day and dragged night in behind it. The new star grew bigger than the sun, then blotted out half the sky. The worker felt a great heat and vanished from the Common Place, dropping Pala Ai into darkness. The sharp disconnect stunned the Queen.

Before she could recover, the colony leapt. The Queen flew for a moment before impacting the ceiling, feeling the rough, untrodden earth against her soft flesh and hard chitin alike. She rolled and slid along the ceiling to slam into a wall. Eggs bounced everywhere around her

35

as drones clung to the earth, only to have it break off in their feet and mandibles. She reached out, but could do nothing to stop herself. Her body was too large now for her weak, useless legs. Pala Ai ended up wedged into a corner, dirt falling onto her, eggs striking her, as the shaking ebbed but did not stop entirely. Drones regained their feet. She relaxed and focused her mind into the Common Place.

Damage reports came in from all over the colony. Tunnels collapsed, and dozens of mold farms and detritus chambers and their occupants left Pala Ai's perception. She didn't have hard data, but she could feel the probability of the colony's survival plummeting. What was happening? She tried to poll her workers and drones, seeing what they saw, getting a grasp of the full scope and cause of all this damage.

Fragmented chaos flooded the Common Place, usually the picture of harmony. Aswarm with input from spinning, tumbling drones and workers, the Queen had a hard time focusing, organizing the information. Earth freed from walls and ceilings bounced around, clogging tunnels. Other viewpoints simply vanished. Pala Ai's sense of the overall form of the hive, gathered from the positions of her subjects, like knowing the position of one's limbs without looking, was thrown off. It seemed the hive was spinning, broken, but what could cause this? Another event unseen, unrecalled by ancestral memories. These were momentous times, but would the colony live to pass on these memories? Would she?

Heat flared, as it had when the scout vanished under the looming star. The outermost chambers became unbearable so quickly that only a handful of eggs were saved across the whole of the colony. Workers scuttled as quickly as they could to the main shaft and down, toward their Queen. She could feel the nascent minds in the more advanced eggs crying out as the heat cut through the loose tangle of languid sensations for one crystalline moment of agony before they faded out of the Common Place.

What was happening? An attack? By whom? She saw no other creatures, smelled no new smells but those of burning and fear. She sent a worker fleeing from the mold farms upward to the entrance. Here, too, the heat was unbearable, but the worker pushed on as best it could. A strange, orange light was the last thing it saw before succumbing. The temperature continued to rise. The workers arriving in the Queen's chamber with eggs deposited them and went to work shuffling and beating wings to create airflow. It helped, but it was only noticeable because she felt workers in outlying areas continue to drop as the heat grew.

"Oh great Mothers!" she prayed, calming herself to a deeper state, like the Common Place but one where she was the recipient, the one awaiting command, counsel. "Nothing I have seen, nothing you have passed to me has prepared me for this. What is happening? How may I save my children?" The jostling and increasing heat around her body dragged her away before she could get any answer, if there was an answer.

As inexplicably as it had come, the heat faded, leaving more collapsed tunnels, blocked by slick surfaces too hard to dig through. Pala Ai sent workers to dig around these blockages, parallel to known tunnels. These ran into soil packed so hard it could not be dislodged. As they worked, high, sharp cracking sounds were heard throughout the colony. They were small, frightening sounds she could not tie to any creature or event. The workers scraped their mandibles thin trying to break through the worrisome soil.

The excess heat vanished as quickly as it had come, then continued to flee, bringing the colony to winter temperatures in hours. Outer chambers that had been so hot became frigid. Frost formed on charred eggs and destroyed mold plots. Workers seeking to salvage food from the latter retreated and joined the Queen in her chamber, which was becoming quite full.

The dancers of course were working at a different job now, vibrating, turning their bodily energy into heat to keep them all alive. The air became thin. The Common Place grew difficult to hold onto. The Queen dozed and dreamed, briefly, of a great colony spanning hundreds of hives, under trees and berry bushes and past streams which never ran dry. She dreamed of summer until she dreamed no more.

...

Pala Ai's domain skipped along a new atmosphere. Its passengers frozen in its gut, it cracked in the sudden heat of atmospheric friction, shards shearing off and burning away. Heat thawed the core. The final, tiny, shooting star of Pala Ai's empire struck water. The glassy, charred outer surface exploded, expelling Pala Ai and her retinue into the waters. Mold spores, leaves, all floated in a sea of organic chemicals. Ions reacted with ions. DNA partially replicated, enzymes remembering their jobs even after so long. Bubbles of polysaccharides and proteins formed, faint memories of the creatures to which they'd once belonged.

In time, bubbles bonded with bubbles or were absorbed by others. Guts and mouths and eyes evolved, a faint copy of a damaged template, wriggling through the water, hiding in strands of green algae, or waiting for prey to reveal itself. A million iterations, attempts for surviving snippets of DNA to continue to survive, a billion. So many forms swimming, crawling, flying.

Nayasal burrowed down into the rich soil, alone, for now, but bursting with urgency. She dug and scraped straight down, excavating a chamber in which she finally lay, expelling eggs which clustered around her. Her spawn grew within. Her mind dropped down, caressing each of them and letting them know she was there for them, to watch over them and guide them.

## *Mother of All*

She was the first Queen in a new line, but somehow she didn't feel alone. Sitting in the dark, Nayasal dreamed. In those dreams she saw trees with strange bark and oddly shaped leaves, but they were somehow familiar. She saw one blue sun in the sky, rather than a yellow one and a red one. She felt waves of heat and cold, of the world turning upside down and panic flooding through more minds than she could conceive of. She woke in the dark, disoriented, but familiar smells replaced the odd ones clinging to the fog of dream.

Dropping down into the place she now knew was called the Common Place, Nayasal wove the shards into a new narrative. The handful of daughters who attended her saw the goddess Pala Ai ruling in the world above, wisely, her colony growing. In battle, she led her legions against demons of fire and ice. In her final sacrifice, she descended from the heavens and brought life to the world. This was the legacy each new Queen would pass on to their daughters, the path of sacrifice each would try to emulate. Someday, when their reigns were over, they would join their mother and the goddess in the heavens, shining in the night sky for all to watch in wonder.

### ###

## About the Author

John A. McColley lives in a vortex of worlds, characters, machines, and language, constantly dragging images and forms out of the storm onto canvas, paper, or computer screen to share them with others and give them new life. When not wrestling with words, he cranks dials and makes sparks at his local hackerspaces and searches the wilds of New Hampshire for semi-precious stones with his wife and son. His work is currently available in *Crossed Genres'* first issue of the year, various anthologies, and at *Mad Scientist Journal.* He's got an author page on Facebook www.facebook.com/pages/John-A-McColley/105420682981117 and a twitter account @JohnAMcColley.

He'd love for you to visit his blog at http://johnamccolley.wordpress.com/.

*****~~~~~*****

# The Shamrock Award

by Jennifer R. Povey

The odds were against us from the start.

Well, not quite from the start. They were against us from the point at which the drive malfunctioned and tossed us into deep space, far from any of the regular shipping lanes. When that happens, you have only so long to fix it.

Or you're dead. I knew we were dead, and from glancing over at Carla's pale face, I knew she knew it too.

Unless we could get the drive fixed. Survey partners are very carefully chosen. Most of us end up as lovers, sooner or later. In the early days, they'd fought that tendency. Sent out two straight men or a gay man and a woman or some combination that wouldn't end up in the sack.

They'd all gone nuts. So, we were lovers, me and Carla, had been through training. It worked. Humans needed that intimacy. She was short, bright, vivacious, lots of curls. Nobody thought we were together. They still thought one of us had to be the "man," those people.

Now I saw all of the life drained out of her. We knew the risks. We knew the odds, always against us. Not many survey teams retired. Not many partners survived the loss of the other.

Usually it was like this would be. Went out, didn't come back, lost somewhere in the void of space. They'd tried robots. Robots didn't have the right initiative. Had to be humans, had to be partners.

"Okay. Carla, you know your job."

She nodded and started to clamber aft. She was the better engineer—and also the smaller of us, by far the better equipped to crawl around the drive and work out what was wrong. Mcmillan drives were complicated and simple at the same time. I didn't pretend to understand the principles.

I just flew the things. Out, back, sometimes spending a year on a single world. Humanity needed worlds. Oh, we didn't breed as fast as we once did, but longevity didn't help lower our numbers. And we needed worlds that didn't belong to anyone. Interstellar war wasn't something you, well, did. We'd learned that lesson. There was an entire genre of movies back in the twentieth century where scrappy humans beat off incredibly technologically advanced aliens.

Yeah. Just cast us as the aliens. I shook my head. I had to concentrate. The worst part was that we could live for weeks before the air systems needed to be renewed. Out and not back.

I turned my attention to the scanners, while Carla checked the drive. And discovered the odds were in our favor after all.

...

It wasn't much of a planetary system. Yellow dwarf star and only three planets. Maybe it hasn't had much good dust. Maybe the outer planets had all been torn away, because the outermost of the three was about in Earth's orbit.

And Earthlike. I let out a soft whoop, and turned all of our sophisticated scanners on the little orb. Gravity assessed at about point eight, standard oxygen-nitrogen atmosphere. Which meant life, because you couldn't have that kind of atmosphere without carbon-based, oxygen-breathing life. And photosynthetic life. Plants. And animals. Which meant we might be able to survive down there. We had rations for months. We could possibly renew the air scrubbers.

Either way.

"What is it?" Carla's voice, through the intercom, muffled.

"Earthlike planet. Easy reach. We're the luckiest women in the entire universe." I was already changing course. Even if we got the drive fixed, this one wasn't on the charts. We could just as easily survey it as any other.

"Not our target star?"

"No. Yellow dwarf. But it's an unreported system, because it's small. No gas giants, only three terrestrials, largest is just a bit smaller than Earth. Small wonder it got missed." My worst fear now was that the world would turn out to be inhabited by just the wrong kind of civilization.

Primitives, you could easily avoid. People with the star drive or close to it you could talk to and trade with, even if they were a bit xenophobic. What we dreaded in survey was coming across planet-spanning civilizations that only just had space travel, or didn't.

That's what we wanted to see the least, because you couldn't sneak past them, and half the time they'd shoot you as soon as look at you. Primitives might mistake you for local deities, but, again, you could avoid them.

So, I was scanning carefully for radio emissions. Civilizations before the danger phase didn't have radio. Civilizations after it tended to slowly wean away from using it as they discovered that it was much more efficient to turn their communications into light and send them through tubes.

Nothing. No radio emissions. That meant primitives, nobody, or they were so advanced we'd be worried about them, as it were. Just because we hadn't found a "weirdly advanced" civilization yet didn't mean they didn't exist. Some even thought the absence of evidence was evidence of presence.

More likely this world was pre-technological or uninhabited. We hoped for uninhabited. Then we could plant Earth's flag, and Colonial would come after us to assess it really, really thoroughly. We didn't start sending colonists until a world had been observed for several local years.

Yeah. We'd learned that lesson too. More than once. But for our purposes. . . for giving us time and sanity to fix the drive, it would work.

I started to head for orbit, planning on doing a couple of circuits before finding a good place to land.

. . .

Broken drive or no broken drive, we followed all of the pre-landing procedures. Carla had re-emerged and pronounced it a "tricky" fix. She recommended landing, but I was still appropriately cautious.

If there were sentients here, they were still in the hunter-gatherer or similar stage, or aquatic. Aquatics we tended not to worry about. We'd shared Earth with them for generations—and we'd learned a lot since then. The Annova colony was one of our most successful.

So, I was not too worried as I set the ship down. Survey ships can handle most atmospheres. . . not gas giants and nothing highly corrosive, but everything indicated this was normal.

And when we finally tested the air and opened the door, the first thing we heard was bird song.

Well, something song. Might be avians, might be insects, might be the local equivalent of mice. There was something heartening about it, though. This planet was welcoming us.

"Okay. So, we work on the drive, and we survey this place." I pulled Carla into my arms, kissed her briefly. "Maybe we'll get this year's Shamrock Award."

The Shamrock Award was a survey pilot in-joke, given to the one with the best, worst, or weirdest luck in any given year. There wasn't a trophy. The prize was a giant cookie shaped like a shamrock. When you live on rations as much as we do. . .

"If this place is any good." She grinned back at me. "Then we deserve it."

44

A drive malfunction dropping us onto a usable world would not be a first, but it had only happened a couple of times. "Let's get started."

The air had already been thoroughly tested for toxins and pathogens that might affect humans, or we'd still be in pressure suits. Still, part of our job was to catch unknown pathogens. That's one reason teams didn't always come back. The first thing we had done on landing was set a warn-off.

If we didn't turn it off, it would stay there and nobody would land here. It would be assumed the world had got us, somehow.

For right now, we set up all of the rest of the sampling gear. Carla walked over to a tree and carefully tugged off a leaf. The stem leaked milky sap.

"Watch that. It's either delicious or poisonous." Or possibly both, depending on how it was prepared.

She sniffed the leaf and sneezed. "Both!" she exclaimed. "Capsaicin. Whewf!"

I laughed a bit. "Watch out, that means there's large browsers around." Plants didn't bother with things like capsaicin unless there were grazers to deter.

"I know what I'm doing," she mock-grumbled at me, studying the tree some more.

We'd sleep on the ship. Always safest that way, at least to start with. Night biting insects had driven people off of more than one otherwise attractive planet. Sometimes you could repel them.

Sometimes, not so much. Night here, though was odd.

Everything went silent.

On most planets, especially uninhabited ones, the beasts became noisier once darkness fell. Not here. It was like there were no nocturnal critters at all. Which bothered me. There were patterns life took.

If nothing was moving at night, then there was a reason for that. So, for now, we didn't move at night.

...

We did move during the day. We would spend the morning working on the ship and the afternoon exploring, and then reverse it, but we were always careful to be back before dark.

No. We were terrified, and we clung together in the darkness. We put on white noise, but there was the knowledge that nothing went out at night.

Why?

Flares from a nearby star that had caused problems in the past, fried the nocturnal animals, and scared the others? Other than the lack of nocturnal beasts, the ecosystem seemed healthy.

There were even multiple candidates for domestication, including the sugar glider like creatures that had welcomed us with their song. Humans needed animals almost as much as we needed each other.

But the nights were silent. Eventually, I could stand it no longer. I was an experienced surveyor. I was not going to let a bit of quiet scare me into submission.

Leaving Carla sleeping where she lay, I headed out into the night.

It was very dark, my torch the only light. People who live their entire lives on settled worlds don't always know how dark it is when there are no cities on the entire planet.

This night was pitch, the stars shining through it. No moon—this world had none. It was also cold, colder than I thought it should be.

Then I heard it. A sound. The first sound I'd heard at night on this world. It sounded like a child being strangled.

On Earth or Earth-stocked worlds I would have known it instantly. Cougar. Except it sounded a lot bigger than a cougar and, somehow, more rhythmic.

So. There were nocturnal creatures after all.

46

I started to back away toward the ship. Whatever had made that feline scream might easily mistake a human for prey.

Then the night went completely silent again. Something snapped, and I ran for the ship, far more afraid of the silence than of the screams.

Right outside the ship I stopped, caught my breath, and turned to face the night again.

And saw it. A silent shadow, many times my size, larger than any predator had a right to be. I saw the ruler of this world's night. It wasn't a deal killer. Humans could deal with such creatures—as a last resort by expelling them from our cities and leaving them preserved wilderness to walk.

No. It wasn't. But when I saw what it was carrying, I fled into the ship. "Is the drive fixed?"

Sleepily, Carla looked up at me. "Yes."

"This planet's a bust. Get us out of here."

I wasn't sure we would make it, though.

The giant predator had been carrying a gun.

A very large gun.

### ###

## About the Author

Jennifer R. Povey is in her early forties and lives in Northern Virginia with her husband. She writes a variety of speculative fiction, whilst following current affairs and occasionally indulging in horse riding and role playing games.

This is Jennifer's second outing with Third Flatiron. Her story, "Whimper," appeared in the anthology, *Universe Horribilis*. She has sold fiction to a number of markets including *Analog, Digital Science Fiction,* and *Cosmos* and written a handful of RPG supplements, some of which are available from Occult Moon Publishing. She also writes comic books. Her first novel, *Transpecial,* was published by Musa Publishing in April 2013.

*****~~~~*****

# The League of Lame Superheroes

by James Aquilone

**Conference Room 3, Hilton Garden Inn, Staten Island, New York**

"Guys, I'm not going to sugarcoat things," Harold said, opening the twelfth annual meeting of the League of Superheroes. "We had a terrible year—even by League standards. According to my records, we failed to save the world seventeen times!"

Harold hoped for a response along the lines of "Holy cow, we suck," or "We're so ashamed of ourselves, Harold, please forgive us," or "Seventeen times? Really? Maybe we should try harder before we all become Professor Edison's mindless slaves." But as usual the League disappointed him.

"Woo-hoo! A record!" Steve shouted, lifting both his arms straight up over his head like a referee signaling a touchdown.

Jesse smiled. "Boy, we're damn lucky the All-Star Champions of the Multiverse are around. Remember when Mr. Superlative lifted the Chrysler Building and flung it like a spear at Edison's mechanical Cthulhu?"

"While I don't often agree with their crude hero ethos, I have to admit the All-Stars are awesome," Veronica added, gazing at Harold with the scrutiny of an X-ray machine. It made him feel weird.

"They are *not* awesome!" Harold shouted, and slammed his fist down on the table. After picking up the notes that he'd knocked to the floor, Harold said, "The All-Stars are a bunch of over-muscled, over-hyped freaks. I can't believe they're considered the good guys. I'm pretty sure they take hero-enhancing drugs."

Harold shook his head. Seven years as the League's leader, and every meeting went like this. No wonder they never saved the world. "I really can't believe this, guys. *We* could save the world. *We're* heroes too, you know?"

"*Lame* heroes," Steve said. "That's what everyone calls us, including my wife and kids. It's embarrassing. I don't even tell anyone I'm a hero. I say I'm a telemarketer."

"Maybe they will call us something different—*when we save the world—once—just once!*" Harold stopped. He loosened his tie and began fanning himself with a sheet of paper.

"Drink something," Jesse said.

"I'm sorry, guys." Harold took a sip of water. "But I know we can be awesome, too. It's all in my notes."

"Yeah," Steve said, "but our powers just aren't—"

"—powers," Jesse finished.

"The All-Stars have real abilities. We have weird quirks."

"Powers are overrated," Harold said.

Sure, their abilities weren't as flashy as the All-Stars', but they were still useful. There was Jesse, Likeable Jesse: Every person who ever met Jesse adored him. Harold thought it was the kid's smile. It was a really nice smile. Steve, The Lucky Dog: He had a mysterious knack for not doing anything he didn't want to do. Usually it was mowing the lawn or doing the dishes, but sometimes it got him out of some tough binds. Veronica, The Noticer: The newest member of the League noticed things no one else did. She killed at "Where's Waldo?" And then there was Harold, The Boss: His entire life people put him in charge of things—student councils, homeowners' associations, bake sales.

"Then why haven't we ever saved the world?" Veronica asked.

"Because we've been going at it the wrong way. My new three-point plan will turn things around. Belief, Teamwork, Knowledge. I call it BTK."

"Wasn't that the name of a serial killer?" Steve asked.

Harold glared at Steve, and then he began his pitch. "One, Belief: Being a hero is all about confidence, right? We need to believe in ourselves. Two, Teamwork: On most of our missions, you guys act like orphans in a bouncy house. We need to work as a team. Three, Knowledge: We need to learn from the All-Stars. I know I don't care for them, but they've saved the world countless times."

"Four hundred and seventy-two times, to be precise," Veronica said.

"Thank you, Veronica. That's why I invited a guest speaker to join us today."

"Oh, you didn't invite that lunkhead Mr. Superlative, did you?" Veronica asked. "Or Barbara Bombshell? She's set womanhood back a thousand years. I swear her body is structurally unsound. And, please, someone buy her a pair of freaking pants."

"It better not be Ultra-Violent Boy," Steve said. "That kid's unstable."

"It's not anyone from the All-Stars," Harold said. He removed a round metal device from his briefcase and placed it next to the complimentary glazed donuts in the middle of the conference table. He pressed a stud in its side, and a three-dimensional hologram of Professor Edison flickered to life.

"Greetings, lame heroes!"

Steve jumped out of his seat. "Edison? You invited the most dangerous man on the planet to our secret meeting? What were you thinking?"

"First of all, it's a hologram," Harold said. "Second, the meeting was not a secret. I posted it on Facebook. Third, he promised no funny business. Sit down, Steve."

"Great move, Harold," Steve said, as he sank back into his chair. "*This* is why we're lame."

51

"Not lame, just unsuccessful. And we need to take drastic measures. Edison promised—and I believe him—that he only wants to talk about the All-Stars. I think we can learn how they've been so successful."

"Not successful—lucky," Edison said. The supervillain stood barely five feet tall, but his shiny black boots gave him another six inches. He wore a dark blue cape and a white porcelain mask. "Your leader is correct. I mean you no harm. And taking our past run-ins into consideration, you mean me no harm."

"Not nice, man!" Jesse said.

"My apologies, Jesse. I should reserve my ire for the All-Stars. They have been quite a thorn in my side. Still, they don't deserve the respect lavished upon them. Their PR department should get the credit."

"I know we aren't getting the full story from the media," Harold said. "Any insider stuff you can share with us would be great. For instance, how did they stop your army of killer robot marmots?"

"There was an unforeseen vulnerability in their design that those do-gooders stumbled upon. Thousands of the creatures were burrowing through all the major cities of the world. The All-Stars could never have stopped each *individual* robo-marmot. But they were all connected to a network. The All-Stars needed only to destroy the server, and all the marmots were rendered inoperable. That's what you get when you hire minions from Stanford."

"And your Moon of Doom?" Veronica asked.

"Budget issues defeated us, not the All-Stars. We were already five trillion dollars into the project when we began to run low on funding, so we skimped on the shielding for the core reactor. The Stanford guys said, 'don't worry about it, it's all good.' Yeah, right! All it took was one lucky blast, and the entire thing blew up."

Suddenly Edison stopped, threw open his cape with a flourish, straightened, and, in a booming voice, said, "Does anyone know what time it is?"

"Good thing you brought that up," Harold said. "We probably have to give up the room soon. It's 2:46."

"Splendid. If someone would be so kind as to check the news on his or her smartphone. The story should be out by now."

Veronica was the first to find it. "Holy jeepers! The All-Stars are gone!"

"It says they were killed during a rescue mission in Siberia!"

"By an anti-matter bomb!"

"Edison!"

Edison shrugged. "That is the true reason why I agreed to come today. I wanted to be with you when the news broke."

"To gloat?" Harold asked.

"No, to *rejoice.* I know you hate the All-Stars as much as I. That is because I was once one of you. Behold. . . " And with that Edison swept off his mask, revealing a scarred and twisted face.

"Little Eddie Kline? We thought you died when your artificial sun exploded in your grandmother's garage!"

"Well, my me-maw nearly killed me, but I was just left badly burned. My inventions, though brilliant, always caused harm. As a lame hero I was one of the lamest, but as a villain I reign *supreme.* I destroyed the All-Stars! Join me. We can show them all what a bunch of lame-o's are really capable of!"

"We will never join you," Harold said. "We have all made a pledge to defend the weak and the innocent, a pledge we mean to keep. And nothing will—"

Just then the hotel manager popped his head into the room. "Ladies and gentlemen, we're going to need this room for the Girl Scout Jamboree meeting at three. If you can start clearing out now, that would be swell. Feel free to take the donuts with you."

"Sure," Harold said. "We're done here."

The manager gave a thumbs-up and left.

"Regrettable," Edison said as he placed his mask back on his face. "But before I go, I will give you one more piece of information. My latest invention is called the Negatron. It is a *marvelous* application that will broadcast a very nasty piece of audio to every electronic device, television set, radio, etcetera, etcetera. Anyone who hears it will be instantly seized by the deepest, darkest *depression*. Sadness will spread across the planet like a virus. None of my test subjects lasted more than two minutes before committing suicide. The Negatron goes live in one hour. So long, lame asses!"

Edison's image flickered and went out.

"Time to save the world, guys," Harold said, rising. "Now, does anyone know where Edison's lair is?"

...

**Underneath the New York Public Library, Midtown Manhattan**

The subway tunnel was dark and stank like pretzels and falafel covered in garbage. It wasn't an unpleasant smell, Harold thought.

The League stood before a steel door set in the wall, holding up their cellphones for light. Veronica examined the door with unblinking, Arctic-blue eyes. Then, suddenly, she said, "There's a tiny stud on the wall." She pressed it, and the door swung open.

"Good noticing," Harold said.

Finding Edison's lair wasn't difficult. Steve had roomed with Eddie at his underground pad when they were both in the League. But Eddie kicked Steve out when he refused to put the cap back on the toothpaste after brushing his teeth. Fortunately, Eddie didn't change his address.

They stepped into the narrow, musty tunnel. The sound of dripping water echoed against the stone walls, and rats squeaked in the dark. Harold was feeling pretty satisfied with the team as they marched down the passage. This was already the closest they had ever come to saving the world. Usually by now someone would have stubbed a toe or lost his wallet or broken down in tears and they'd have called it a night.

When they entered a dimly lit room cluttered with wooden crates and discarded electronic equipment, Veronica stopped and held up a hand.

"Someone's coming," she whispered.

They ducked behind a stack of gutted Commodore 64s and iMacs.

Footsteps rattled in the distance. They grew louder, and then stopped.

"Whoever's here, I have a pulse gun!" a voice shouted.

"Jesse," Harold whispered, "work your magic."

Jesse stepped out from behind the crates and approached Edison's minion. He immediately raised his pulse gun.

"Freeze!"

"Hey there, bro," Jesse said, and flashed a smile.

"Oh, hey." The minion lowered the gun a fraction, and returned the smile. "Are you lost or something?"

"Or something. I don't want to bother you—nice uniform, by the way—but do you know the way out of here? I'm trying to find the Number 7 train."

"You must have taken a hell of a wrong turn."

Jesse's chestnut-brown eyes lit up. "Wow! Is that a real pulse gun? I've only seen them in comic books."

The minion grinned. "Pretty cool, huh? You want to check it out?"

"Oh, man, I don't know."

"No, go ahead. You seem like a nice guy."

The minion handed over the gun.

55

"Sorry about this, bro," Jesse said, and trained the weapon on him. "All clear!"

The rest of the League suddenly appeared behind Jesse.

"Where's Edison?" Harold asked the minion in his best tough-guy voice.

"I'm not telling you."

"Where's Edison?" Harold asked in his second-best tough-guy voice.

"I'm not going to tell you just because you asked me twice. Do you think I'm an idiot?"

"Jesse?"

"Where's Edison, bro? We just want to talk to him. It's cool."

The minion's stern expression melted, and a smile slowly spread across his face. "OK, I'll take you to him."

The minion led them down a winding staircase, over a moat filled with mutant sewer alligators, through a series of hidden doors, and finally to a landing that overlooked Edison's control room.

"Just go down the stairs at the end of the landing," the minion said.

"You've been awesome," Jesse said. "I don't know how to thank you."

"Maybe we can catch a Mets game sometime. I have season tickets."

Jesse grinned—and then he bashed the minion in the face with the butt of the gun. He went down like a bag of dirt. "I might be a lame hero," Jesse said, "but a Mets fan?"

"I noticed an open broom closet back down the hall," Veronica said. "We could stash him there."

"Steve, take care of it," Harold ordered. "But first get those magnetic handcuffs off his utility belt."

"Sure."

Harold crawled onto the landing and peeked over the railing. The control room was crowded with computers and odd-looking machines, the sort of machines an insane five-year-old would make if his only toys were circuit boards and Lincoln Logs. Edison stood in the center of the room facing a large computer screen. Two minions fluttered about as Edison barked orders. An electronic display beside the computer screen was counting down the time till the Negatron's transmission. It was at 00:09:03.

As Harold was thinking of a plan, Edison shouted, "The jig is up, lame asses!"

Each League member wore an expression that said "Oh, crap." One by one they stood.

"Jesse, give Steve the gun," Harold whispered.

"Good thinking," Steve said, and took the gun.

"Put down the gun, or my minions will vaporize you!" Edison ordered.

"I don't want to do that," Steve said, and marched slowly down the stairs.

"Like when you didn't want to put the cap back on the toothpaste! You were always so inconsiderate. Take another step, and you're dust."

When Steve reached the bottom of the stairs, the second minion drew his molecule-eroding pistol, fired, and—

Nothing happened.

"Goddamn! Is that the *prototype* molecule-eroding pistol you're using?" Edison growled. "What is wrong with you Stanford guys?"

"Lucky Dog!" Jesse whooped.

Steve fired the pulse gun. A wave of purple light hit the minion in the chest. He fell to the ground, twitching like a frog on an electrified fence.

"Don't worry, guys. I didn't kill him!" Steve shouted as the minion went limp. "I set it to 'stun.' At least I think I did. If not, then he's dead. Sorry!" Steve glared at the other minion, and he ran out of the control room.

Just then Edison pressed an oversized button set in the wall beside him, and a tube of transparent thermoplastic swooshed over him.

Steve walked over and tapped on the tube.

"You can't touch me in here," Edison said. "The Tube of Isolation is impervious to all weapons. ICBMs, Scud missiles, dark-matter cannons. . . "

Steve walked over to the button in the wall, pressed it, and the tube rose.

Edison ran, but Steve was on top of him in an instant. He knocked him to the ground and clamped the magnetic handcuffs over his wrists. "Just so you know, I was meaning to work on a remote control for the tube," Edison said, as Steve dragged him toward the League, who were now all gathered by the giant computer screen.

"You're too late," Edison said, struggling to his feet. "The Negatron goes live in three and a half minutes."

"Veronica, you're good with computers," Harold said. "Stop the Negatron."

"I use a PC. This is a Mac."

"This is your lame plan?" Edison asked, before throwing back his head and laughing.

"Just *believe*," Harold said. "Remember BTK."

"The serial killer?" Edison asked.

"Just try, Veronica."

In a blur Veronica's fingers danced over the keyboard. She looked up at the screen.

"INVALID OPERATION," the computer intoned.

"Try using voice commands."

"Remember," Steve said, "all Edison's other doomsday devices had glaring vulnerabilities. It's always something simple. Don't overthink it."

"Computer, end current operation," Veronica said.

"REQUEST DENIED."

"Computer, override program."

"REQUEST DENIED."

"Computer, shut down."

"REQUEST DENIED."

"So lame," Edison said, rolling his eyes.

"We have only ninety seconds!" Jesse cried.

"You cannot stop the transmission," Edison said in a bored voice. "You've lost. Once all the networks are found and the audio file is uploaded, the entire world will be plunged into the blackest depression. I hope you all have Prozac."

"Thank you!" Veronica shouted. "He always talks too much. It's bizarre. We cannot stop the *transmission,* but maybe we can *change* what it transmits. Computer, select new audio file!"

They waited, but the computer didn't respond.

"Computer, select new audio file!" Veronica repeated.

A few long seconds passed. Then the computer said, "PLEASE BE PATIENT AS I LOAD THE LIBRARY." A beat later a menu listing hundreds of audio files appeared on the screen.

"Hurry, there's only twenty seconds!" Jesse said.

"Computer," Veronica ordered, "select, uh, select—Edison, you have some crappy songs on here—select Hall and Oates' 'Kiss on My List.' "

"STUDIO VERSION OR LIVE?"

"Ten seconds!"

"Studio version!"

"Nothing's happening, Veronica!" Harold said.

"Damn, I didn't say, 'Computer'—"

"Five seconds!"

"—Computer, studio version!"

"I can't believe this," Edison said, shaking his head. "I really have to start hiring minions from MIT."

The computer pinged. There was a brief pause, and then the room filled with the smooth, soulful voice of Hall or Oates. Harold didn't really know. He was more of a Bruce Springsteen fan.

59

Steve ran around the room, whooping and shouting and high-fiving his teammates.

"You did it!" Harold said to Veronica.

"No, we *all* did it," she corrected. "*Teamwork.* BTK, right?" Veronica gazed at Harold with those too-blue eyes, and for once he didn't mind.

Suddenly an explosion jolted the control room. The back wall crumbled, and through a cloud of dust and smoke, Mr. Superlative stepped into the lair, followed by Barbara Bombshell and Ultra-Violent Boy.

"They're not dead!" Jesse shouted.

"Apparently not," Mr. Superlative said. The ground shook as he strode toward the League. "The anti-matter bomb was a dud. We would have been here sooner, but Bombshell got frostbite while we were in Siberia. I had to use my superlative breath to defrost her."

"Wearing pants might have been a better idea," Veronica muttered.

"What was that?" Bombshell asked. She wore a black G-string, pasties, and, incongruously, a bomb suit helmet. She must have been the one who blew up the wall. Her touch was explosive.

"Oh, I said, 'Nice G-string. It accentuates your nakedness.' "

"Thanks."

"Edison planted the story of our demise in the gossip blogs," Mr. Superlative explained.

"Apparently they'll publish anything," Edison added.

"Well, we've got everything under control here," Harold said, and watched Mr. Superlative's muscles ripple under his suit. Harold sucked in his gut and made a mental note to start hitting the gym.

"I see. Nice job. But we'll take Edison and his minions off your hands now."

"They're ours," Steve said. "We stopped them."

"Do you guys have an anti-gravity prison on a remote island equipped to hold an evil genius?" Ultra-Violent Boy asked. He leaned against a wall covered with flashing green and yellow lights. Pistols hung from both his hips. Strapped to his left leg was a Bowie knife and strapped to his right was a stiletto.

"Not yet."

"Let him go," Harold said. "We've done our job."

Steve shoved Edison toward Mr. Superlative, who handed him off to Bombshell. She and Ultra-Violent Boy swept out of the lair.

"You saved the world," Mr. Superlative said. "On behalf of everyone, thank you."

"Just doing our job," Harold said, trying his best to mimic Mr. Superlative's stentorian voice.

Mr. Superlative nodded stiffly. "By the way," he said, "we're starting a West Coast version of the All-Stars. I think you're just the man to head it up. What do you say?"

Harold smirked. "I appreciate that, Mr. Superlative, but my loyalty rests with the League."

"Good luck, then, League of Superheroes," Mr. Superlative said, before bounding through the demolished wall.

"Did you notice he didn't call us 'lame'?" Veronica asked. "Just plain ol' 'heroes.'"

"I think I'm going to cry," Harold said, and then he did. Like a boss.

### ###

## About the Author

James Aquilone lives in Staten Island, New York. His fiction has appeared in *Weird Tales Magazine, Bards & Sages Quarterly,* and *Cast of Wonders.* His non-fiction

*Astronomical Odds*

has appeared in *SF Signal, Shock Totem,* and *Den of Geek.*
Visit him online at jamesaquilone.com.

\*\*\*\*\*~~~~~\*\*\*\*\*

# *Casualties*

by Martin Clark

*Fortunate is the man who can foretell both the time and place of his death*

My wingman vanished in a soundless flare of light, nova-white against the black of space. He'd given no warning of an attack or systems failure, but if there was an enemy out there I had only seconds to react. I took a last deep breath and opted for transference. My virtual cockpit shimmered.

*Upload complete.*

I cut power to a minimum and fell back on passive sensors, cooling my hull to match the background void. The explosion would have temporally blinded any electronic observer, but a continued telepresence link would negate any attempt at stealth. While my physical body remained safe back aboard the Augusta, I was now one with the Talon combat drone; a mesh of mind and biotechnology.

*Neural net degradation in three hours fifty-nine minutes.*

But as they said, it wasn't habit forming. I felt the tickle of a tight-beam communication across my aft hull and re-aligned the comms array.

"I repeat, this is Augusta flight control calling Talon two-two-one. Hangfire, do you read?

"Augusta, this is Hangfire."

"Hangfire, what the hell just happened out there? We've yanked Snowman from his rig and—"

The voice disappeared in a blare of electronic gibberish.

Silence.

63

I waited, but there was no further communication. Instead I detected a pulse of incoherent radiation, a pulse large enough to signal the death of the Augusta and everyone aboard. Including myself.

*Neural net degradation in three hours forty-five minutes.*

There was nothing I could do. A suitably equipped medical facility could support a noncorporeal intelligence until a suitable donor body became available, but I was shit out of luck. The Alliance was stretched thin out here, and the Augusta had been on her own—more intelligence gathering than looking for a fight. It would be days before Command Interstellar dispatched a probe to see what had happened, let alone risk another ship.

I drifted alongside the cloud of debris from Snowman's drone. The Talon had no jump engine of its own, meaning I was marooned here in Shangdu, an uninhabited system. I didn't even have a self-destruct option. Short of crashing into a planet, all I could look forward to was the electronic equivalent of Alzheimer's.

*Neural net degradation in three hours fifteen minutes.*

My last meaningful act would be to leave behind a record of events. Unfortunately, there was no guarantee a voice recording and sensor log would ever be found. The Talon didn't carry an emergency transponder and was *designed* to evade detection. The chances of my floating hulk being discovered were slim at best.

According to my mission briefing there was a former colony in this system, on the only habitable planet. Actually, calling it a colony was a misnomer, as it was little more than a rich man's retirement paradise. Viktor Ghent, its highly idiosyncratic owner, and his staff had been killed by a biological weapon—rumoured to be the result of corporate infighting. Since then, the place had been off limits, and even scavengers gave it a wide berth.

## Casualties

So, Shangdu had been left to rot all these years, uninhabited and forgotten.

However, the eventual after-action investigation might check it out, regardless. If I could get there and put down in one piece, there was a chance the Talon would be recovered, and with it my posthumous report. I checked my remaining fuel, calculating the flight time.

*Singularity detected.*

A cloaking field collapsed less than three thousand metres to port, revealing a medium-sized merchantman. It was what the Heimat Unity used as a "cruiser"—a civilian cargo hauler retrofitted with whatever second-hand military hardware they could scavenge. That shouldn't run to anything as sophisticated as a cloak, but the separatists were regularly fielding equipment way beyond their meagre industrial and technological resources. Command Interstellar suspected collusion with one or more of the industrial cartels, war profiteers seeking to keep the conflict alive for as long as possible.

An Alliance fighter jock in my position would have attacked immediately—a Kamikaze run, all guns blazing—but I hesitated. Hell, I wasn't even a real pilot, just some nerd who spent his time plugged into a virtual reality flight simulator. I'd been conscripted straight out of college to make good our losses in conventional manned fighters. These days telepresence drones like the Talon were just about all that Alliance carriers had left.

I sensed a radar sweep by the cruiser and offered up a prayer to the God of stealth technology. No missile or other ordnance came my way, so it was safe to assume I'd been overlooked, at least for the moment. The enemy ship hung in space, framed against a gas giant. It was a boxy spindle, surrounded by the twin rings of an early model *n*-space engine. As I watched, the rings began to counter-rotate, spinning up a jump field.

Running an external engine like that restricted sensors to directly fore and aft, along the axis of navigation. Only military vessels went to the ruinous expense of internal generators so as to retain situational awareness until the last moment. The spatial distortion field blossomed, leaving me electronically deaf and dumb.

But not blind.

I'm not a brave man, or even all that patriotic. For me the Alliance was just *there* while I was growing up, and the dissident frontier worlds barely rated a mention amongst "other news." Now Earth was gone, and the bad guys were beating the crap out of us across 20 star systems. Friends of mine had gone off to war and not come back, so maybe I felt the Unity owed me some payback.

I brought up the power, twisting to approach the cruiser from amidships. The distortion field intensified, making me feel sick to my nonexistent stomach. It was like walking while drunk, with that peculiar swaying sensation as if you were balanced on tubes of cotton wool.

This close in, my targeting array was useless, a blizzard of static. I had little sense of scale as the enemy ship filled my field of vision.

*Weapons Status—Armed.*

A Talon carried only six missiles, better suited to sparring with another fighter than taking on an interstellar heavyweight. I paired them up, giving me three target points in line of sight; the clockwise ring and the post side access doors. First strike to knock politely, second to step inside. Any weapon powerful enough to destroy the Augusta had to be an ersatz spinal mount housed in the main cargo bay.

Neural net dysphasia felt like fingernails scratching on the inside of my skull. Being this close to a jump engine wasn't something anyone could tolerate for long, be they organic or synthetic. The rings began to rotate faster, now surrounded by a pale blue hue.

*Weapons Status—Launch sequence complete.*

## Casualties

I spun and soared away on full power, red-lining the engine. Fuel levels were in free fall, but that was the least of my worries. Visual perspective remained dead astern, locked on the enemy.

*Detonation confirmed.*

All I could make out was a brief flare on the engine ring, almost lost against the building jump field. Graviton-generated St. Elmo's fire rippled along the spinning ring and down onto the hull. I registered radiation spikes, the soul-sucking void of an emergency dampening field, the—

White.

Not just a bright or blinding light, but the total obliteration of all other sensory input. I plunged into a dazzling limbo, where even my scream was just another wavelength.

Black.

...

*Hard reboot in progress—Please stand by.*

Systems returned one by one. Some primaries were out, but the Talon was hardened against radiation, and the ship remained viable. Lucky me. Rear sensors were fried, so I spun around to take a look-see.

*Idí ná khuy!* There was a rad zone over a klick wide, shot through with debris and fusion hot-spots. Zero chance of survivors, which I guess made our little skirmish a draw.

*Neural net degradation in two hours fifteen minutes.*

I flew across the bright and hollow sky, approaching a small blue-white marble, a veritable Earth in miniature. It grew to fill my field of vision as I plunged into the upper atmosphere, closing down most external sensors. Drones lack a permanent heat shield, getting by instead with a spray-on ablative skin. Less than ideal, but sometimes you just have to roll the dice. . .

I made my approach vector deliberately shallow so as not to put the heat skin under strain. I rotated to spread the thermal load, although that also raised the chances of finding a bald spot. Roll those dice again. . .

The Talon punched through the ionisation layer into the upper atmosphere, a hypersonic dart aimed at the ground. I extended my wings, trading speed for manoeuvrability. The virtual altimeter started unwinding at a fearsome rate, as my avionics completed their adjustment to this new environment. I'd only flown in a simulated atmosphere before, and the real thing was a mind-numbing jumble of vibration, gravity, and sensory overload.

*Flaps ten.*

*Radar to ground search mode.*

*Variable geometry hull to automatic configuration.*

I pulled out of my dive, flying along a tree-lined valley beneath the level of the surrounding hills. My visual perspective was overlaid with a 3D contour map and ranging data.

My head hurt.

The former colony lay directly ahead, in the centre of a natural amphitheatre. I swept up and over, registering buildings, a circular landing pad, vegetation encroaching on the perimeter, no signs of damage.

*Air brakes active.*

*Flaps full.*

I pulled up sharply, experiencing G forces that would have killed a human pilot.

*Stall warning, stall warning, stall warning.*

*Thrust to VTOL mode.*

*Undercarriage extended.*

I hovered, kicking up a blizzard of dust and plant debris. My wheels touched down, and I cut power, airframe settling into ground mode.

*Engine shut-off confirmed.*

*Radar to standby.*

## Casualties

*Neural net degradation in forty-five minutes.*

More than enough time to compose my report, although doing so now seemed so terribly final. Once it was lodged in the Talon's core memory, I'd literally have nothing to live for.

*Proximity alert.*

It was designed to prevent me side-swiping ground crew and would only be triggered by a moving man-sized object. There weren't supposed to be any animals on Shangdu. I reactivated my external video feed to see just what the hell was out there.

A young woman approached through the dust cloud, moving with the languid gait of a catwalk model. She was slim, of average height, with auburn hair worn in an unfashionable bob. My unexpected meet-and-greet stopped in front of the nose and stood, hand on hip, looking up at where the cockpit would be on a manned fighter.

"Identify yourself." Her voice was calm with a sultry undertone.

"This is an Alliance telepresence drone, but. . ." I broke off, mentally snaking my head. "I'm Maxim Konev, or what's left of him. Formally human, but now just a machine-based intelligence. I'm pleased to meet you, although the circumstances could stand improvement."

"What is your purpose here?" Not so much calm as icy.

"Look, I'm not here to cause any trouble. I just need someplace to lay up, someplace my fighter will be spotted when the Alliance swings by. I've got less than two hours coherent thought remaining, so it's not like I'm moving in."

There was a pause. "Welcome to Shangdu, Maxim Konev, or what's left of him."

*Servitor request.*

Servitor request? I didn't see that refueling would do me any good, but I figured it best not to refuse local hospitality. Multiple feeler arms rose from the landing pad and closed in, like the not-so-tender embrace of a giant spider. I registered connections to my hull ports, and several diagnostic routines kicked in. That made me uneasy, as by rights no civilian tech should have been able to interrogate Alliance hardware.

*Switching to external control.*

The ship dissolved around me, systems vanishing until I was left in a featureless pearl-grey limbo. I tried to scream but had no voice.

*Neural net shut-down in progress. Goodbye.*

...

The world was a silent video screen at the end of a long, dark corridor. The picture was of hands gripping a balustrade and beyond that a view of trees, hills, blue sky, and clouds. The image began to expand, or perhaps I fell towards it. There was no sensation of movement, no sense of scale. I couldn't look away and had no eyes to close.

The taste of burnt copper.

The smell of wet leaves after rain.

The sound of a woman's voice.

"—try and move. Just stand there, use the rail for support. Take a few deep breaths. The sensory interface alignment is intuitive, but that's not to say the process won't make you feel as sick as a dog."

She was outside my field of vision, but I couldn't work out where. Hands twisted my unresisting head so that I faced the redhead. She smiled. "Better? Or at least less shitty? Try to speak."

Words set off but fell by the wayside long before reaching my tongue. My lips moved, seemingly of their own volition. "What?"

"You're alive, Maxim Konev, or what's left of him. My name is Rachel." Close up, she had dark brown eyes and a nose that looked broken but expertly reset. Rachel held up a small mirror. "The implantation took longer than anticipated, but that was to be expected given the neural mismatch." She smiled. "Welcome to your new body."

The reflection wasn't mine; it wasn't even close. "Who?"

"Viktor Ghent. Well, a clone of his body, aged thirty-three. He intended to occupy it once the original was no longer fit for purpose. It came out of cryo storage in perfect condition." Rachel stroked my cheek. "Luckily for both of us."

"You? His wife?"

She laughed. "God, no! There were three unfortunates who took up that particular burden during his lifetime, but I was spared that, at least. No, I'm an Uber-Leben cybernetic companion, comprised of an organic brain in an otherwise synthetic body. Ideal for BDSM relationships."

So her nose had been repaired, not reset. I moved my jaw, getting used to the feel of new teeth. "Been here since? Alone?"

"Well, apart from the house AI. His name is Hugo."

I managed to turn my head and get a better impression of my surroundings. We were standing on a balcony, overlooking a broad sweep of immaculate garden. Behind me were a concertina of glass doors, folded back to reveal a living space in a style fashionable some 20 years ago. A series of outbuildings lay off to the left, and beyond them my Talon sat on the landing pad. All the visible structures showed signs of wear and tear but had obviously been well maintained. "You've been busy."

Rachel smiled. "Me? With these fingernails? No, the maintenance crawlers survived *Gotterdammerung*. They cleared away the bodies—"

"Bodies?"

She tossed her hair. "Oh, all the organic staff. When Viktor died, the house systems released a viral

71

agent that killed everyone else here. One final act of spite by the man, and I really should have anticipated it."

"But this body, he planned to prolong his life."

"Which is why I murdered him before he had the chance to transfer into it, of course."

I stared at her. "What?"

"It was either that or endure decades of abuse." Rachel set aside the mirror and gazed into my eyes. "I was subject to behavioural imperatives, a form of cybernetic slavery. I had to obey Viktor and tolerate whatever he did to me. He insisted on a model with an organic brain, one with active pain receptors. Believe me when I say that he was truly inventive, raising torture to an art form. No living woman could have survived what he put me through."

Shame by proxy left me floundering. "Look, Rachel, I'm sorry. I don't know what—"

"Then my wetware was hacked, removing all ethical and moral restraints. I don't know who was responsible—a business rival, a disgruntled ex-wife, the Pope—and I don't care. It allowed me one brief, *glorious* act of revenge, and I have no regrets."

I frowned at her. "You could have sent out a distress call. No one could have accused you of having killed Ghent, given you're a cyborg operating under the Three Laws. So why remain here all these years?"

Rachel smiled, but there was sadness in her eyes— a masterpiece of simulacra. "Hugo would have been lonely. Besides, as you pointed out, I'm a cyborg. At present I'm possessed of a truly independent intellect and want to remain that way. Hugo shut down the tachyon relay, but if I left Shangdu I'd be exposed to wetware updates and revert to nothing more than a submissive plaything. I didn't go through all this merely to exchange one master for another."

72

"But don't you—". I broke off as the faint sound of the Talon's engines reached me, "What the hell are you doing? You can't fly that thing."

She shook her head. "There must be a ship in orbit. It looks like your friends have come to retrieve their lost property."

I could have run down there so that the drone registered my presence. I could have found a radio and sent off a distress call. I did neither of these things. Instead, I stood and watched as Talon two-two-one lifted off, hovered briefly, then rose rapidly into the clouds and was lost from view. I let the Alliance consider me a casualty of war.

Rachel took my hand in hers. "There is everything on Shangdu to sustain you indefinitely." She squeezed my fingers. "Body and soul."

I looked at the sky, I looked at the garden. I looked at Rachel—and smiled.

There were worse places to play dead.

### 

## About the Author

Third Flatiron welcomes Martin Clark back for a second go. His story, "No Ravens on Mars," appeared in the anthology, *Redshifted: Martian Stories.*

Martin is a freelance writer and occasional poet. He contributes to several online publications, primarily Mythaxis.co.uk. His range of subject matter includes science fiction, urban fantasy, romance, and westerns. He puts this down to the somewhat eclectic mobile lending library where he grew up. He is author of *The Dead Don't Weep* series currently being published by Eggplant Literary Productions.

*Astronomical Odds*

He works as a local government officer in south-west Scotland and is also an evil stepfather.

*****~~~~~*****

# Nick Budapest, Investigating Actuary, in

## Good Odds for Murder
by Iain Ishbel

Predictions are tough to make, with dames. From the look of her legs as she walked through my door, I knew this dame would be trouble. But I also knew the odds were good the trouble would be worth my while. I didn't need my interface to figure those odds—call it a job skill, or maybe an occupational hazard. Ten years as a numbers shamus, I get a feeling about the odds, even before I look at the real data.

But I'm a professional, so I always look at the data. I opened up the IDAT interface. The world stopped moving and turned a dark red. Freezing the world isn't as useful as it might sound, if you ever happen to deal with violence. Your body freezes along with everything else, so there's no way to dodge a bullet. But you can stare at it for a while if you want, and think deep thoughts. Your head works just fine while you're linked into the deep, deep numbers of the data store.

Which is the point. It's like this: think of a spreadsheet like you use for taxes. That's data in two dimensions, and if you know what you're doing you can maybe see the patterns. If you concentrate carefully, you can add a third dimension, like a giant tinker-toy grid, and there's a lot more to see in data like that, if you can keep your head around it.

Some people, not very many, can hold a fourth dimension of data. They can make a good living interfacing with IDAT, hunting down valuable correlations nobody ever saw before. The big airlines, say, pay a lot for 4-D data mining, and the brokerages too.

One time, when I really had to, I held six.

That's how I make a living, as a private investigator. I can find patterns other people can't. Sometimes I find patterns the big corporates don't want found, which is why I have two artificial kneecaps, a plastic rib, and a titanium pin in the bones of my thumb.

...

It wasn't clear what kind of trouble this dame was bringing me, but I knew how to find out. While the world stood still and dark red, I put together three easy dimensions of data about the woman standing in my office, and yes, one of them included the shape of her legs. I had a strong feeling this woman's looks were part of the problem. Sure enough, the correlations were clear: according to the data, she was likely to be trouble, but lucrative trouble. I came back out of the interface and smiled.

"Come in," I said, and gave a nod to my one available chair. As she swayed toward it, I studied her.

There were contradictions. Her hair was blonde, but the colour was genetic, not from a bottle. She wore a skirt of sophisticated dark wool, but it was tailored to hug her hips pretty close. Her shoes—well, never mind the details. Her appearance was saying two things at the same time, which is more unusual than you'd think. She sat, and I heard her nylons sliding together.

"Mr. Budapest?" she asked.

"That's what it says on the door," I said. "What kind of trouble are you in?"

She was startled, but hid it pretty well. She probably thought she was good at poker. "Perhaps I'm here for some business research?" she said, and I sighed.

"Look, lady, you didn't come downtown to hire an idiot, and I don't get paid by the hour. Let's skip straight to the part where you cough up. You never worked a day in your life, but you know how to marry well, so you've got a husband can afford an interface. If you're not going to him for help, then either you're in trouble, or he is."

Give her credit, she didn't try to pretend. Either she was more upset than she was showing, or smarter. "I wish to find out if my husband is cheating."

The old cliché. I answered slowly. "It doesn't work quite that way."

She shifted in her seat, but didn't say anything.

"Data correlations don't find out anything, except if some facts are true, the odds are good that some other facts will also be true. You still have to figure out what's really happening—this is actuarial science, not some crystal ball."

She still didn't respond—this idea was hard to get across. "Look," I tried, "there's a group of guys who correlate strongly with most of the violent deaths in this city. Somebody shows me a corpse, odds are these guys had a hand in it. Who are they?"

She crossed her legs the other way, and once again I heard the whisper of expensive nylon.

"Well, I don't know, Mr. Budapest," she said. "It sounds to me as though they are dangerous criminals."

"One of them is a friend of mine," I said, "and a hospital nurse. He works emergency rooms." I paused until her face showed comprehension. "One fact may be connected to the other, but that doesn't tell the whole story."

She lowered her eyes. "I hope I haven't wasted—"

"I can still tell you what data is correlated with a professor having an affair."

Her eyes didn't react noticeably, but she did stop breathing. I counted to four in my head before she exhaled again.

"I won't ask how you know my husband, Mr. Budapest."

"I don't know him," I said, "but I'm glad you're not asking. If I gave away all my secrets, I'd be out of business."

"I thought I was the one with secrets," she said, and showed me her best smile. I decided to take the job. I leaned back and slipped deep into the IDAT interface. The world went red and stopped moving. And I may have taken just an extra moment to look at her legs, which, by the way, were spectacular.

The good data wasn't too far away, like always. I started with male academics—after a moment of thought I left out women—and then made a cross-field with registered divorces. I filtered divorce by cause, resulting in a broad plane of primary data: all the academics in the entire world who had, or hadn't, been caught cheating.

Next was the hard part, why people pay for gumshoe actuaries like me to dive into the IDAT. I needed to stretch the data in another dimension, find an indicator that varied the same way as affairs. I tried a few spitballs: surprisingly, body weight didn't correlate, and neither did wealth. I guess I will never understand women. I did notice a strange dark stuttering pattern and for a moment thought I had something, but when I pushed in close, it wasn't what I thought: seems homosexual professors mostly don't have affairs. I'd have to think about that, another time.

That pattern was a dry well, but it's where I got my first lead. Sometimes the thing to do is let your mind wander. For a couple of minutes I let mine go, and it wandered from homosexual professors, to a priest I used to know, to the faculty of divinity (wrong: priests have the same ratio as the rest of the faculty, if you want to know), but then I started thinking about the professor's department, so I looked in on whether that made a difference.

To make a short story shorter: it did. Correlation went through the roof. Law professors are the worst,

78

nearly guaranteed to cheat; then business, English lit, and economists, in that order. There was a big cluster around 50/50, all the humanities, which says some pretty sad things about academics right there. But then it evens out, with a huge gap in chances before you get to medicine, science, engineering. . . all the way down to the astronomers, who almost never have affairs. If you find yourself a gay stargazer, odds are very very good he's sleeping at home.

So when I stretched out the data by department, the slope was very, very steep, and I relaxed a little. It was a good start. As usual, once I had found a way in, cross-correlations didn't take very long, and soon I had another useful dimension, then a third. I slipped back out of the interface and watched the dame's long legs come back to life beneath her dark skirt.

"Okay," I said, "I'll tell you what I know." I named a price, a steep one.

She opened her clutch and took out a slim black tablet. She tapped the surface carefully a few times, then placed it on my desk. We let the devices talk, then I nodded, and she put away her expensive toy.

"A few questions first," I asked. "What does your husband teach?"

"Literary Theory," she said, and I hid a frown.

"Does he play team sports?" I didn't understand it either, but numbers don't lie.

"No. Tennis and running." Another strike against him.

"Do you have any children?" She told me, and this time she caught me frowning.

"Well?" She knew what was coming. "Mr. Budapest, are you going to tell me?"

Wisdom from my friend Reaney in the emergency room is you give bad news fast and clear, and then get ready to say it again. "Odds are he's cheating," I told her. "Over ninety percent."

79

"No," she said, "That's not right." So I repeated it. "That bastard," she said, and stood up. Her chair fell over backward, and I stood up too.

"Look, it's—" I started to say, and then I stopped. There was something in her purse I hadn't noticed before. It had hard corners and a distinctive shape. I didn't know if it was loaded, but who carries an empty pistol?

"Wait," I said.

I hit the interface, hard. I needed ideas, and I needed them soon. I didn't think the answer was anywhere in IDAT, but I had no clue what to do, and I needed some time to think.

Violent crime, court records, psychological assessments, medical data, college sports statistics—all of the disconnected, unstructured information of the Information Age swirled in front of me. Every fact anybody could ever record, combed out and laid down in lines, then those put into a giant line made of lines, piled on top of each other in lines of lines of lines, a volume of lines disappearing into another dimension of volumes—I snapped back into the real world, where the chair was still bouncing on the floor. My mind was spinning now, but I had nothing. My throat was tight, and I coughed. A drink would have helped, but I didn't see how I could reach for the drawer without getting shot.

"See, now, when—when a man's killed in this town, it could be for a lot of reasons. It's a lot to look into. But when a man and his mistress are both murdered, the police know where to start. It's obvious." As I said it, an idea formed in my head. It was a long shot, but that's life in the real world.

"How obvious?" she asked. I looked at her and waited, looking certain, while the idea settled in my mind. Finally she nodded, and took out her tablet again. "Very well, Mr. Budapest. You drive a hard bargain."

"It's not your money anyway," I said, and I waited until she paid. "When a cheat's found dead with the other

80

woman, six times out of seven it's the wife. When there's only one body, though. . . " For a moment I hated myself.

"Yes?" There's no angels, Nick, I reminded myself. It's a tough world, and you've got your part in it.

"One in fifty," I said. "Probably less than that in your case, considering single men get killed too." It hurt to lie, but I sold it as hard as I could.

"Huh," she said, then: "All right. Well. She can. . . " She stopped talking and looked at me. I sat back down and looked out the window. She didn't say anything for a while, just stood there thinking. I opened the bottle from the bottom drawer and poured myself a glass while I waited. Then I watched attentively as she finally turned away, took three long, long steps and closed the office door behind her. For a moment, her figure was silhouetted on the glass, then she was gone.

Once the sound of her shoes had faded away, I tipped the glass back, letting the bourbon burn my throat. I don't like lying to a customer, especially a dame; you can get a bad reputation that way.

And that can lead to hurt feelings. She was going to get caught, sure as trees hit the ground. When they took her in, she'd realize I'd been lying to her. It's always the wife, no matter who gets killed.

But what else could I do?

The bourbon started to warm my chest from the inside, and I supposed it wasn't so bad. I'd saved some girl's life. I'd been paid, twice. And those legs—well. I'd known it was going to be a valuable visit, and watching her walk away had indeed been worth the trouble, all by itself. But I hoped I'd never see her again.

And for that, the odds were good.

###

**About the Author**

      The author is a technical writer and recovering English teacher living on the Pacific coast of British Columbia. In the field of anonymous bureaucratic financial procedures he is well-published, but in fiction only twice: He was the 2013 winner of the Victoria Times-Colonist "So You Think You Can Write" contest, and shortlisted for CBC's Canada Writes "Bloodlines" writing contest.

*****~~~~~*****

# A Clone Called Slick

Garry McNulty

My wife, Elisha, had me cloned. While I was working long hours to pay for her high standard of living *and* an enormous bill for producing her new clone—well, technically my clone—she was home having him do things for her.

In the bedroom. Yes, those kinds of things.

For the record, I'd have been more than happy to do some of those things for her. It's just that I have a very stressful job and I'm really busy most of the time. Of course, Slick had all the time in the world, because he didn't work. Yes, she named him Slick. Personally, I thought Chester II would have been a little more appropriate.

When I'd get home from work in the evening, they'd both be wearing those disturbingly satisfied smiles as we sat around the dinner table. Neither one would think to ask, "How was your day, Chester?" I was certainly not going to ask what they did all day. They might have told me, and how awkward would that have been?

Elisha said it wasn't cheating, because Slick was a copy of me. "It's the same as sleeping with you, Chester, only better, because he's more rested and open to trying new things."

I thought about killing him. It's still illegal to have a clone in the first place, so I don't know what the authorities would have done to me. I have to say the idea of killing a guy who looks exactly like you is extremely creepy. Not to mention how upset my wife would have been.

Slick did like the same TV shows and movies as me, giving us clear control of the TV remote and DVD rental decisions. But that's small compensation for being replaced as your wife's lover.

I finally hit on a solution. I turned to online dating and found Slick a date with a lovely blonde-haired, blue-eyed woman named Cindy. Would you believe he refused to go out with her? After all my hard work.

I didn't want to stand the woman up, so I went in his place. Turns out Cindy and I really hit it off, and we continued seeing each other.

Eventually I told my wife, "Elisha, I'm leaving. From now on you can look to Slick to support you. Good luck to both of you." She was not happy.

Slick, however, handled the news well. He went right out and found employment. As a matter of fact, in less than a year he was making more than me. Elisha was still not happy. She had regained a provider but lost an attentive lover.

So, she ordered a clone of Slick. She called this one Ace. Last I heard from them, Ace was keeping Elisha smiling, while a disillusioned Slick was going online, looking for a mate for either him or Ace, he didn't seem to care which.

I guess that may be the relationship cycle we have to look forward to in this crazy new world. Yesterday I found a Clones-R-Us brochure in Cindy's purse. It's probably just a matter of time before I have to start searching online for a new girlfriend.

### 

## About the Author

Garry McNulty has sold short stories on such websites as Amazon.com, BarnesandNoble.com, and UntreedReads.com and sold short, short stories to *Flash Fiction Online, Insatiable,* and *Untied Shoelaces of the*

*Mind.* In addition, two of his screenplays have placed as finalists in national scriptwriting contests.

Father of two wonderful daughters, Kelly and Erin, Garry resides in Melbourne, Florida.

*****~~~~~*****

# Time's Elastic String

by Nick Slosser

Colonel Astor relieved Major Ngaio at the controls of the Lightship Frontier, bidding the major a dreamless sleep. Before exiting, the major related a story he'd experienced through Diderot—the ship's central nervous system. The story was about sea stars in a tide pool.

"Back at the turn of the century," Ngaio said, "a kid at some Canadian university visited some tide pools to video the organisms there."

"On celluloid?"

"No, they had digital by then. Anyway, I stood right here with the waves moving around me—trying to be there, you know—and I watched. . . for hours. The sea stars did nothing."

The colonel nodded. "As I recall, they weren't known for speed."

"Exactly. But this kid had a real brainflash and videoed them using time lapse. Played back, what he got were chase scenes like the old-time ones around waterholes in the Serengeti. But instead of lions chasing zebras, it was sea stars chasing sea urchins."

"Really?"

"And it was exciting! The sea star sticking right behind the sea urchin, hounding its prey as it climbed over rocks and down and around the seafloor. It was a life-and-death chase, except that watching it with the naked eye, you couldn't tell what was happening, because to us they're hardly moving at all."

"That's interesting. You really like those nature files."

The major nodded. "Seems to me, people have forgotten all we've lost."

"Perhaps. Then again, some people seem to prefer I-tech to reality."

"Immersive technology doesn't even compare."

"Really? Weren't you sitting on a riverbank in the Yukon the other day, watching polar bears eating salmon? Couldn't do that in real life, could you?"

"It was grizzly bears in Alaska. And no, I couldn't do that, because there are no grizzlies anymore. And no salmon either."

The colonel nodded. "Not outside of a lab, anyway, at some sim-food conglomerate."

"There's only one conglomerate left. The one we work for. The one everyone works for."

"Good point."

"Thanks, but getting back to my original point: imagine being a sea star going about your business at your own pace, only to have some kid scoop you up and shake you around and rip your arms off, before tossing you willy-nilly back into the sea."

The colonel frowned.

"Talk about a glitch in the matrix."

"Don't know that one."

"Seriously? You don't know a glitch in the matrix?" Ngaio said.

"Or willy-nilly. What language are you speaking?"

"Willy-nilly means carelessly, haphazardly. And a glitch in the—never mind. Who cares. There aren't any sea stars anymore."

"Not outside of a lab."

The major nodded, his brow creased. Then, as if coming around to the elephant in the room, he said: "So, we should be 3 hours, 46 minutes to the next slingshot event."

"Thank you, Major."

"This one's a black hole."

"I'm aware of that."

"Of course. I just meant. . . should I come back?"

88

"That won't be necessary, Major. It's just another gravitational field. You need rest."

The major stared, trying to find a way to allude to the strange events surrounding their other encounters with black holes without relying on words like supernatural, paranormal, extranormal, or freakazoidal.

He chose: "It is advisable to look from the tide pool to the stars and then back to the tide pool again."

The colonel waited for an explanation.

"Steinbeck. Goodnight, Colonel," he said, although the odds of him sleeping were orders of magnitude less than than the odds of him teleporting back to Earth using only the power of his mind.

"Goodnight," the colonel replied.

...

The first black hole event should have been taken as a warning: Stay away.

Astor had been "sitting at the controls," a mostly *pro forma* occupation, since Diderot, comprising the ship's navigation, data processing, and immersive technology subsystems, actually performed all the necessary decision-making and navigation. Diderot automatically sought out the next celestial body—planet, degenerate star, black hole—within a few degrees of their inertial vector and set the course.

As Frontier approached the object, it performed a flyby, utilizing the object's gravity to slingshot itself through space. Sailing unimpeded through a frictionless void, Frontier also converted cosmic rays to energy, until the lightship eventually reached its current speed, within a thousand kilometers per hour of the speed of light, nearly 300 million meters per second.

The crew of three, in rotating eight-hour shifts, were merely observers, guarding against the unlikely event that something might go wrong and require human intervention. Indeed, their employer—a global conglomerate so monstrous it didn't even have a name—

calculated the odds against such an event as too large for most government-issue home processors to even approximate.

Still, the crew kept to the cyclical schedule, the colonel relieving the major, the major relieving Grand Inquisitor Majmudar—titles which were, in fact, meaningless and changed often—as Diderot's nearly limitless databank of I-tech programs made adhering to the schedule as painless as not. The first black hole flyby had landed on Astor Khan's shift.

Astor Khan, who suffered from motion sickness, preferred less immersive programs than Surgeon-General Ngaio—self-appointed after successfully removing Sheriff Majmudar's ingrown toenail. Astor Khan favored cooking shows from the early 21st century, before the First and Second Corn Collapses and Universal Seafood Ban, wondering how smoked salmon, strawberry shortcake, or vine-ripened tomatoes would have tasted before genetic optimization and sim-tech.

Sometimes, though, while the others slept, she secretly watched *telenovelas* from the late 1900s. About twenty minutes before the first black hole slingshot event, with one eye on a heavy-handed but stylish program, she noticed her sim-café changing location and boiling without a heat source. Assuming she was hallucinating, she froze the program and tried some deep breathing.

Minutes later, the hull of the ship began to expand and contract around her. But it wasn't until she saw things through the viewport—moving, writhing things—that she got spooked and alerted Surgeon-General Ngaio and Sheriff Majmudar, who corroborated her experiences. Even Diderot seemed to have gone haywire.

These strange phenomena reached their peak at the moment of tangent or periapsis—the point on Frontier's hyperbolic trajectory when she was nearest the center of the black hole—then quickly began to dissipate. About an hour later the extranormal activities ceased entirely.

...

The second black hole event, which had landed on Emperor Majmudar's shift, was much worse. Starting half an hour before the event, the hallucinations began similarly, but grew more intense and freakier as the moment of tangent approached. There was also a "presence" on the ship that everyone felt but no one could explain, and a rotting stench with no tangible source. And then Majmudar vanished, leaving behind only his scream.

With the bulk of the ship being dedicated to propulsion, life support, shielding against micrometeoroids, and housing Diderot's massive databank and processors, searching the livable space—sleeping quarters, common area where crew members ate and took their exercises, and cockpit—took exactly 13 seconds. Majmudar was gone.

"What the hell is going on?" Ngaio demanded.

"I don't know," Astor said, "but we have to get clear of this black hole. Can you override Diderot?"

Ngaio stood there stupidly, hardly comprehending her question, still trying to grasp the reality of Majmudar's disappearance.

"Cardinal!" Astor said. "Focus. Can you override Diderot?"

The cardinal blinked and said, "I'll try."

"Well, do it, man."

Cardinal Ngaio tried, accessing Diderot through one of three manual ports, but found the task extremely difficult given the extent and complexity of Diderot's programming. Indeed, at several points, Diderot seemed to sense the Cardinal's intent, and kicked him out altogether. . . with apologies.

"It's not working," Ngaio said. "Diderot keeps overriding my override."

Astor nodded. "Of course it is. Why would the company trust us to fix it?" She sat down, as objects around her defied the basic laws of physics, wondering how she'd gotten there.

Like all great adventurers—Hanno the Navigator, Xu Fu, Ericson, Magellan, Cook, Shackleton, Amundsen, Earhart, Yeager, Cousteau, Laika, Ham, Gagarin, Glenn, Tereshkova, Armstrong, Cameron, Kiri-Moss—the crew had launched into the void with no guarantee of returns or returning.

But like musicians without melodies or misers without money, explorers without uncharted frontiers might as well starve, for nothing that has already been trodden upon, mapped, christened, and claimed-in-the-name-of could possibly fulfill an appetite for the unknown.

Astor and the crew of the Lightship Frontier, however, were not explorers. Once agents of high-tech corporate espionage, the crew had been blackmailed into volunteering.

Outlawed by the very mega-corporation who had employed them to steal their competitors' sim-tech—thus ensuring their employer would subsume its competition to become the only game in town (read: the world)—the crew had reluctantly chosen endless spaceflight over lifelong incarceration. They'd chosen wisely, considering prisons had long been a privatized industry, most of which were owned and run by that same nameless employer. Incarceration in the private sector would most likely mean being secretly experimented upon. . . for profit.

The Lightship Frontier launched on August 4, 2062.

It was now, on Earth, 2199. Astor, Ngaio, and Majmudar had aged maybe twenty-five years—it was hard to tell. The jump to near light speed didn't happen instantaneously, as it did in the old celluloids, but gradually in fits and starts.

Frontier's mission: classified. Diderot took care of all data collection, analysis, and transmission. But these were corporate spies, not scientists, so even if they'd been briefed on Higgs fields, gravity/gauge duality, nonlocality, and M-theory, they would not have grasped their significance.

And by the time the data they were gathering reached Earth, the crew couldn't be certain that TASA—the Trans-Atlantic Space Agency, the astrodynamics research arm of their nameless employer—would still exist to receive their transmissions. Or, for that matter, the American-European Economic Union. Or even the human race.

As the futility of their situation became all too clear, they reached the moment of tangent, and the hull around her threatened to collapse like an empty sim-beer can. She eyed Ngaio helplessly. For his part, the cardinal had curled up into the fetal position and repeated the word, "Mommy," until it became one relentless string of syllables, "Mommy-mommy-mommy-mommy," with no beginning and no end.

That's when Majmudar reappeared.

At first, all they heard was a faint whimpering, which they both chalked up to the unnatural phenomena occurring around them. But as the moment of tangent sped away behind them, Astor recognized the difference in quality that meant the whimpering might actually be real.

"Ngaio."

"Mommy."

"Ngaio!"

"Mommy-mommy."

"Cardinal!" growled Darth Astor the Master Blaster.

"What?"

"Do you hear that?"

"No-no-no-no," the cardinal said, threatening to embark upon another endless string.

"It's Majmudar."

Astor reached Majmudar's bunk first.

"Where were you?" she asked, kneeling by his side.

Majmudar trembled and eyed her like a pounced-upon rabbit.

"Emperor, what happened?" She took his hand, which seemed brittle and shapeless, and he screamed. She let go.

Behind her, Ngaio peered through the hatch, but kept his distance. Majmudar, whose jet-black hair now showed streaks of white, merely lay there, uttering a pathetic, canine whimper.

Horrified, Darth Astor the Master Blaster shrank from the room.

"What the hell is that?" Ngaio demanded.

"I don't know."

"What the hell is going on?"

"I don't know! Any question you ask, the answer will be the same: I don't know, I don't know, I don't know, *ad infinitum*. Okay?"

The cardinal nodded.

Meanwhile, Frontier seemed to have forgotten its misbehavior and acted as though nothing had happened.

"We need to check the logs," Astor said.

Ngaio nodded.

"So check the logs."

Ngaio nodded and, like a voodoo zombie, moved torpidly to no apparent purpose.

"Do it, man," she said. She could have done it, but she needed Ngaio focused and alert.

The cardinal regained his composure. "Diderot: playback, non-immersive, video-to-monitor, audio-to-drum, today's date, 0350 to 0520. That should cover it."

Diderot: "Yes, Cardinal. Playing back 0350 to 0520."

Ngaio: "Also, list environmental and life support readings, same time-frame."

Diderot: "Listing."

Ngaio: "Also, run internal-diagnostics, check 0350, 0435, and 0520, itemize hull integrity."

Diderot: "Running."

Astor: "Why didn't we do this the first time?"

Ngaio: "Maybe because nobody had vanished the first time, and then reappeared all broken."

Astor nodded. "I thought Diderot had just gone glitchy getting so close to the event horizon—you know, cracking some immersion file that felt phantasmagorical or something."

Ngaio looked at her. "What is today's date anyway?"

"Here or back home?"

"Here?"

She shrugged. "Lost track."

"Back home?"

She shrugged again.

Meanwhile, Diderot had already finished compiling the data, which it listed on three screens, along with audio-visual playback on a fourth.

"There's nothing unusual here," Ngaio said. "Environmental and life support readings within normal ranges, internal-diagnostics the same, even hull integrity normal."

But Astor was preoccupied with the playback, which was no less horrifying for engaging only two of the senses. The scene played like an old horror celluloid, the kind where a family has decided to record the strange and unnatural happenings in their home, thus pissing off the spirit or demon inside, instead of just grabbing the kids and running the hell away. . . far, far away.

And once again the futility of their situation came crashing down upon her: there was nowhere to run to; no far, far away to go hide in. They were stuck in a flying trash can—albeit a stubbornly intelligent trash can—light-years from home, with zero control over their own lives.

"We can't do this again," she said. "Before the next black hole, we need to convince Diderot to avoid it."

The cardinal nodded.

Easier said than done. Diderot would not be convinced. And after working on the problem for six weeks straight ship time, they quit trying. Meanwhile, Majmudar had rejoined the rotation, though he would not speak of his experience during that second black hole event. Indeed, none of them would.

Instead, following the advice she'd once seen in a histo-doc on World War II, Astor had resolved to "keep calm and carry on," to focus on the present. Only in private with the lights out did she pray that their trajectory through the incalculable vastness of space would not inevitably aim them toward another black hole. She might as well have prayed to win a lottery without buying a ticket.

...

Colonel Astor scanned the instrument panel. They were still 2 hours from the slingshot event. Major Ngaio and Grand Inquisitor Majmudar were in their bunks. Majmudar did not look well. He was aging fast, his biological clock broken.

Although he'd logged off, the major had left Diderot's immersion subroutine fired up. Perhaps he thought it could distract her. But what the colonel needed was the one thing Diderot, with all of its archives and all of its simulators, could not offer: an escape plan.

"Diderot: power down immersion subroutine."

Diderot: "Yes, Colonel. Powering down."

Sitting in the dark, with only the thin blue light of the instrument panel to illuminate her features, she waited for the approaching slingshot event. Whatever happened, it wouldn't be the immersion program glitching. It would be real.

She pictured Shackleton waking up on Elephant Island, having to summon the reserves to disregard his

96

own fear and desperation—if indeed he felt them—because it was his responsibility to lead his men.

But what was the point? Shackleton was trying to get his men home. She was not. The odds of returning home, even if they could turn the ship around, were infinitesimally small. And for what? Everyone they cared about was already dead.

She set those thoughts aside. They were exactly the breed that a Shackleton would not abide. Sitting taller, she raised her chin, eyeing the upcoming event. She now recognized the void within a void that marked a black hole. Behind her, through the open hatch, she could hear Major Ngaio alternately praying and whimpering. Grand Inquisitor Majmudar remained strangely tranquil.

The happenings began, as they had before, with what seemed like hallucinations. But this time they ramped up much faster, the fleeting apparitions growing rapidly more distinct and grotesque. And the "presence" had returned.

With her heart in her throat and her mouth dry, she waited, willing herself to remain calm, to carry on. Behind her, a blood-chilling scream followed by silence told of Ngaio's fate. Perhaps she'd be next. Or perhaps not. It was out of her hands. . . a roll of the dice. . . a spin of the wheel.

She was approaching the moment of tangent when the temperature suddenly dropped, and the entire ship flickered and faded around her. Her body lost its stomach as it would in a swiftly descending elevator.

Time itself contracted. She saw her own lightship from the outside, but only vaguely, like a spectral afterimage. And she saw the ghost of herself inside the lightship, watching through the viewport. She felt a searing pain, as if her body were being stretched and torn apart then smashed back together, over and over again.

Still, it wasn't until she lay in the common area, unable to move, drifting in and out of consciousness, accompanied only by unspeakable agony, that she realized what was happening. And in answer to the cries she heard coming through Ngaio's open hatch, she whispered:

"Sea stars."

### 

## About the Author

Nick Slosser lives in Portland, Oregon, with his wife, daughter, and cat. There he spent ten years slinging books at the Rose City's only independent all-mystery bookshop, Murder by the Book, until it closed its doors last April. He now works a job not worth mentioning and writes. Nick's stories have been published at *Shotgun Honey* (shotgunhoney.net) and *Blood & Tacos* (www.bloodandtacos.com).

*****~~~~~*****

# Lost in the Mail

by Benjamin T. Smith

Idril, the Post Mistress for the City of Besnaffer, smiled at me from behind her oaken desk. "How can I help you, Mr. —?"

"Adelvell," I said, trying to hide my frustration behind a smile of my own. "I sent two letters from this posting house a week ago, and they never reached their destinations."

"That is troubling." Idril cocked her head to one side. The gesture tinkled the tiny bells hanging from her helix caps (all the rage amongst the urban-dwelling elves). "How important were these letters?" she asked.

"Enough that I paid the extra silver to get them certified, with tracking runes included." I ground my teeth for a moment. "One was my licensing fee to the Summoner's Guild headquartered in Merriley.

"The other was the down payment for a lab in tow. The closing was to be yesterday, but the bank in Ashmeadow told me the sale was suspended until they received my check."

"What day were these letters delivered here?"

"The ninth."

"You brought them?"

"No, a familiar of mine did. Uluran," I called. The shade materialized behind me and peeked over my shoulder at Idril, a frightened look on her pale face. "She's a bit shy," I apologized.

Idril shook her head, the bells ringing in time with the fervent motion. "This may explain why my magical sense has been particularly sensitive since last week. It's not every day a veil-piercer enters my posting house."

"Hey," I objected. "We in the industry prefer the term 'planar transient.'"

"Of course. My apologies."

"I instructed her to keep the letters together and get them here safely, which she did." I reached over my shoulder and patted Uluran on her glowing head.

"You said these letters have tracking runes?"

"Yes." From my robes I withdrew a symbol-covered piece of vellum. The inscribed runes were supposed to change as the associated letters reached new points along their route.

Idril accepted the document and muttered an incantation. The runes flared to life, pulsing a brilliant yellow. The Post Mistress studied the light's rhythm for a moment before speaking. "There are only two status marks for either letter. Both originated from this office, and both entered processing. That is, they both went into the Machine."

That sounded ominous. "The Machine?"

"The sorting apparatus in the back." Idril smiled. "The dwarves and gnomes who maintain it treat it with a bit of reverence. We all do, for that matter. It's the device that allows us to function as well as we do."

I bit back a retort, instead asking, "Does that mean that these letters never left this location?"

The helix caps sang as Idril shook her head. "Not necessarily. These two marks are generated automatically, first on acceptance and then upon entering the Machine for processing and sorting. All remaining updates must be performed by the carrier whilst en route, a task many neglect, to our shame." She shrugged. "It's possible that the letters were lost somewhere after leaving here."

She reached for the quill on her desk and pulled a fresh piece of parchment from a drawer. "I'll send out a search request to all posting houses connecting here and the two destinations." She thought about it. "There should be about thirty-two of them."

"Thirty-two?" I was aghast. "Merriley is but sixty leagues from here! Ashmeadow is closer still!"

Idril cast me a sidelong glance. "Carrier pixies do need to rest once in awhile, Mr. Adelvell."

*Little wonder why postage is so high,* I thought. "When do you expect word?"

"A week or two."

"What? Why so long?"

"King's Carnival is the day after tomorrow, and it will last for days. Posting houses around the realm will be closed in observation, so I doubt a search for these letters can occur until after the backlog of the holiday is finished."

I pounded the arm of my chair with my fist. "This is going to ruin me! My clients will go to other summoners, and I'll be on the street!"

Idril smiled patiently. "We're doing all that we can, I assure you."

"Can't you check here for it?"

Her smile faded, and she looked at me quizzically. "Why would we do that? The letters entered processing. That means they were sorted and sent out."

"What if they're caught in the Machine somewhere?"

Idril laughed, the chiming of her bells and peals of her mirth mingling into an infuriating medley of mockery.

"Oh, sir," she said, "that is quite impossible. The Machine has never failed in its centuries' long existence. The chances of one letter becoming stuck are slim, but two letters at the same time? That would be—"

. . .

"'Astronomical,'" I said, recalling Idril's words. "Hmph."

I stood in the shadow of a tree across the street from the posting house. The fortresslike structure had been bustling with activity ever since I stormed out. Customers were no doubt hurrying to get their letters mailed before the carnival.

101

What a ridiculous notion. How was anyone to get any work done with week-long holidays scattered all over the calendar?

I came to a decision as I watched the posting house begin to shut down for the day. Something had to be done. If the letters were lost somewhere else, so be it.

But, if the letters were still here. . .

"Yiltahn," I whispered. "Come forth."

I watched as my shadow warped, expanding and contracting several times before settling to its original shape. I could see nothing, but I felt as if the icy grip of death were near. A voice sounding like sandpaper running over bone spoke directly into my mind:

"Yes, Master?"

"Lend me your form," I commanded, sending the wraith Yiltahn a mental image of the two missing letters. "My livelihood depends upon this."

"Of course."

I closed my eyes and was suddenly looking at myself from Yiltahn's view. Wraiths had no eyes—nor any other organs, for that matter—so their senses were entirely supernatural. It took some getting used to, but I was a master in necromantic summoning. I had worn Yiltahn's form many times.

I left my body in the care of a nervous Uluran and moved towards the posting house with Yiltahn's incorporeal form. Together we passed through the outer wall and soon found ourselves floating down torchlit corridors in search of the central chamber.

Numerous pixies winged their way to and fro, all lugging satchels of mail several times larger than their petite frames. Now I understood why they needed to rest periodically.

I rounded one corner too wide and passed through the chest of a fellow human, who shivered and made a comment about the building's draftiness. I continued on more carefully.

## Lost in the Mail

A large door lay at the end of the next hallway. Once through that I was inside a chamber that could only have been the sorting room. And by room, I mean *cavern*. It was gigantic. The walls and even parts of the ceiling were covered with moving conveyor belts laden with mail. Huge warehouse doors stood open on the far side, allowing wagons to drop off and pick up. There was also an elevator leading up to the roof. A goblin clad in the gloves, goggles, and cap of a gyrocopter pilot stood there, waiting for the overnight deliveries to be loaded.

And there in the center of the chamber was the monstrosity I had been looking for: the Machine. It was a gargantuan construct of polished brass and copper, with more tubes than a pipe organ coming out of it in the oddest of places. Each pipe belched out smoke and steam at regular intervals.

Two shirtless, sweating dwarves wielding shovels stood at the Machine's front, an ever-growing pile of mail next to them. Together, they were dumping hundreds of pounds of letters and packages into the waiting, greedy maw of the Machine.

I had to move fast. Missing letters would be the least of my worries if the Post Mistress or any other magically sensitive employee discovered me. I floated over the heads of the dwarves and entered the Machine. Once inside, I made my way through a veritable stream of paper and cardboard, studying each mechanism or grate that I came across, looking for anything that resembled the missing letters. I passed under an array of glowing crystals, where I assume the mail was scanned for weight, destination, and correct postage amount. Past this, the conveyor belt split into a dozen different directions.

Yiltahn had been primed by my knowledge of the letters, and it was through his ethereal nature that we found them. The letters were inches apart from one another at the openings to separate conveyors. They had somehow become stuck to the wall and would not budge.

To my immense relief, they appeared undamaged, despite the torrent of mail passing by them over the last week.

*Not so astronomical after all*, I thought as I coalesced part of Yiltahn to grasp the letters. They came away from the wall with ease, which was odd. What had held them fast this entire time?

I tried letting them go down their respective belts, but once more they adhered to the wall, less than a foot apart. Had Yiltahn had a mouth I would have been using it to frown. This was most perplexing.

After a few more tries I gave up and decided to bring the mail with me. Perhaps I could leave it on the Post Mistress's desk with a fake note from a subordinate.

No sooner had I reached the mouth of the Machine than I heard a noise that chilled me more than Yiltahn's presence ever could.

The soft tinkling of bells, very close.

Idril was standing mere feet from the apparatus, her back to me as she looked around and sniffed the air. I did not risk moving any closer. I released my hold on Yiltahn's "hands" and became shapeless again. I led my borrowed form up into the rafters and watched as the letters struck the ground next to the Post Mistress.

Idril picked up the letters and looked at them closely. I wished I could have heard what she was saying to herself, but all I could do was watch as the Post Mistress held my very life in her hands and pray that nothing untoward would occur.

...

"What have we here?" Idril asked herself aloud.

The letters were covered with a very thin layer of ectoplasm that only an elf or supernatural being could detect. A tiny strand of the same substance connected the two letters together, and no amount of pulling could separate them. She brought the letters up to her face and inhaled.

"Uluran," she said, recalling the scent of Mr. Adelvell's ghoulish familiar. Was this what she had been sensing for days? It was stronger today, but maybe the letters really had been lost inside the Machine.

With a muttered word she dispelled the ectoplasm from around the letters. She thought about taking them around to the sorting trays they would invariably wind up in. What if they became trapped inside the Machine again?

The Post Mistress shook her head and smiled. That the letters had become stuck in the first place was an amazing event in and of itself. That it could happen twice?

"Astronomical," she said as she tossed them back in.

### ###

## About the Author

Benjamin Smith is a writer of fantasy, science fiction, and anything else that suits his fancy. His work has been published in several anthologies and online publications, including *Kaleidotrope, Chaosium, Fringeworks,* and *Dark Opus Press*. He is currently working on several short stories and even a novel or two, which you can follow at BenjaminTSmith.net.

\*\*\*\*\*~~~~~\*\*\*\*\*

# *Birth Lottery*

Susan Nance Carhart

The receptionist at Dayspring Clinic—a division of Dayspring International—was herself obviously a gene-mod. No Naturalborn could have that perfect skin and that fashionable nose. Her silvery eyes slid in dismissal over the commonplace appearance of the young couple before her, but she acknowledged their appointment, gave them an expensive, professional smile, and gestured gracefully at the waiting room.

"I should have had my hair done," Kerry said, feeling inadequate. "I should have bought a new outfit."

Rob slunk further down in his chair. "Maybe I should have, too."

After doing their research, they knew there was no use coming to Dayspring Clinic until Kerry was already pregnant. The day the test had shown positive was the happiest of their lives. Kerry was only two weeks along, but they were already determined to invest in their child's future. It seemed the *right* thing to do.

Other clients came in and out of the office: mods of awesome elegance with eyes in expensive, trademarked colors: Ancient Electrum, Rainforest Green, Devonshire Violet. They were all tall. They were all thin. Some of them—the second generation mods—looked almost too exaggerated to be human, or at least what passed for human these days. They communicated in quick, liquid voices with the clinic's staff, who were all mods themselves: splendid mods who made brilliant advertising for the clinic's services.

Eventually, Kerry was called in for her tests by a goddess masquerading as a lab assistant. When the samples and swabbing were complete, she emerged, blushing and intimidated, and sat down by Rob, drawing her legs up, making herself as small as she felt.

"Are you all right?"

"Not very. That girl was so condescending!"

They waited. Time passed. At one point, Kerry had the uncomfortable sensation of being watched, and she looked up to see the exquisite clinicians looking her way, talking in low voices. They noticed her attention and walked away. There was another wait, and the young couple dozed in the squashy chairs, lulled by the color and movement in the huge tank of tropical fish and corals decorating the waiting room.

"Kerry and Rob? The doctor will see you now."

Half-awake, they stumbled into a gleaming consulting room, lined with screens displaying pictures and looping videos of developing embryos and beautiful, elaborately modded children.

They waited there, too; they waited for some time. At length, the door slid open, and a remarkably handsome man in a lab coat entered. Kerry was fascinated by his gleaming teeth. He was a mod, too, of course. How else would he have qualified for medical school?

"Doctor. . . ?" she asked, hoping for a name.

"Felix. You can call me Felix."

Kerry wondered if that meant it was not really his name, but some sort of professional alias. "Doctor. . . Felix. Nice to meet you."

He shook their hands with a nicely judged amount of pressure, lit up the room once again with his smile, and then assumed a grave, professional expression. He laid a tablet on the table, pressed it lightly, and scanned the contents, shaking his head.

"Our mission at Dayspring Clinic is to help prospective parents create the best possible future for their children," he said. "You're doing the right thing, coming here. I've had a look at the results, and it's clear that you're just the sort of parents who can benefit most from our prenatal screenings."

Kerry and Rob smiled vaguely. Rob was first to realize that the doctor was not being complimentary. In fact, the doctor was about to launch into their child's undesirable traits: traits that Dayspring Clinic existed to eradicate.

"First of all, you've got yourselves a little girl. Is that a problem?"

"No!" Kerry glanced at Rob, saw his hesitation, and was hurt. There was no way they could afford more than one child. She had not realized that he had really wanted a son.

"No," Rob finally said. "No." He squeezed Kerry's hand, to show he meant it. "I'm fine with a girl."

"Strabismus," the doctor read. He snorted a laugh. "Surely you'll want that dealt with. You wouldn't want your child to have crossed eyes!"

"Of course not," whispered Kerry, hanging her head, knowing that it was her fault. The strabismus came from her side.

"Rob, there's a history of colorectal cancer in your family, isn't there?"

"Uhhh. . . yes," Rob winced. It wasn't something anyone would die of these days, but the treatments could be lengthy and inconvenient.

"We'll have to do something about that. We can't have it hanging over the poor little girl." The doctor ticked off more bullets on the tablet, and then clicked his tongue in alarm.

"Look at this! Galactosemia: you only see this in less than one in 60,000 live births!"

Rob was bewildered. Kerry stammered, "I—I don't know what that is."

With pitying condescension, Doctor Felix gave them a textbook answer. Easy enough, since the text was outlined in pulsing red on the tablet's screen. He paraphrased it with authority, as if he had done the research himself.

"It's a rare genetic metabolic disorder. It's autosomal recessive, which means that *both* of you are carriers," he added, with a look of disapproval. "This child will not be able to metabolize the sugar galactose properly. Galactosemia confers a deficiency in an enzyme responsible for adequate galactose degradation."

"Is there a treatment?" Rob asked.

Doctor Felix looked even more disapproving.

"The only treatment for classic galactosemia is eliminating lactose and galactose from the diet. Without a restricted diet, it's possible the child could experience long-term complications like speech difficulties, learning disabilities, neurological impairment, *tremors,*" he enlightened them, in a sepulchral voice. "There have been cases of ovarian failure in females. As an infant, this child could not be breast-fed, and would need a soy-based formula."

Kerry ventured, "So as long as we don't feed the baby anything with lactose, she'd be all right?"

She wilted under his look of crushing contempt.

"People who allow a child to be born with such a condition are hardly deserving the name of parents!"

He expanded on the diagnosis.

"Two copies of the gene must be mutated for a fetus to be affected by an autosomal recessive disorder. An affected person has carrier parents who each carry a single copy of the mutated gene. You had a twenty-five percent chance of your child being affected by the disorder, and it seems she won the birth lottery," he added, with heavy irony.

He was not done. He paused, studying the tablet, and then gave them the rest of the bad news.

"The child is also carrying a gene for xeroderma pigmentosum, which you only see in one in 250,000 live births. If the other parent of her children was also a carrier, her children would be unable to endure even tiny amount of ultraviolet light."

Rob protested, "But if she and her future fiancé went for genetic counseling. . . And how likely is it that she would connect with another carrier, anyway? You said it was really rare. . . "

The doctor raised his brows, and brought up another picture on the biggest screen in the room.

Kerry and Rob flinched. A wretched child, his skin freckled blue with dozens of basal cell carcinomas, gazed out at them blearily, his dim eyes empty of hope. There was nothing more to be said. The doctor, his point made, changed the image to a benign one of two little girls watching a butterfly. He gave them a slight smile, approving their chastened mood.

"Both galactosemia and xeroderma pigmentosum *are* rare. For a child to be burdened with both these conditions is even rarer. I can hardly guess at it. Maybe one in a million... one in ten million. Combine with it the strabismus, the vulnerability to colorectal cancer, and you have a child that is battling astronomical odds, simply to function in society at all." He sighed deeply, and looked down at his tablet.

Rob swallowed. Kerry's eyes were brimming with tears.

"Well," the doctor considered. "Maybe. . . you'd be better off scrapping this one and starting fresh."

It was an inspired push at their feelings.

"Oh, no!" cried Kerry, crying in earnest. "No!"

Rob pulled her close, pressing his cheek against her rumpled hair. "We're not going to do that," he told Doctor Felix. "Just tell us what we have to do to make this right."

"The Dayspring Clinic will take care of it all," the doctor assured, his smile dazzling as a ice storm. "There's absolutely nothing wrong with your little girl that can't be fixed. All you have to do is sign the contract."

This process took much longer than the diagnosis. There were the genetic problems to be arranged for, and then the doctor led them through an endless array of "Cosmetic Packages," and "Skill Builders."

Bewildered by the images of beautiful children, Kerry could only manage a faint objection. "We *do* want her to look like our daughter!"

"Of course. Of course," soothed Felix. He glanced at them out of the corner of his eye: a raking glance that told them just how damaging that demand would be for a helpless child. He gave them a brave smile. "She will, of course, have your dark hair, Rob, and your blue eyes, Kerry, though it could hardly hurt to intensify the color slightly. People judge each other by their eyes. It's very important that your little girl's eyes be as beautiful as we can make them. Don't you agree?"

Kerry and Rob looked at each other in despair, trying to stop the avalanche. It was hopeless.

"Well. . . I suppose so."

"Wonderful!"

He brought up a picture of an exquisite dark-haired little girl, and began flashing through a display of various eye colors, showing how they looked on a real child.

"How about Imperial Iris?" he asked. "They're very striking with dark hair."

"I don't know. . . " sighed Kerry. "They're all gorgeous. Maybe. . . Indigo Ocean? It reminds me of our honeymoon in Santorini. . . "

"Very nice. Excellent choice."

"Do we have to make her so tall?" asked Rob, looking at the guidelines for the cosmetic package. "She's going to be taller than me."

"Yes, yes," said the doctor. "I'm trying to do this in the most economical way possible for you. These traits are all tied together. If you don't want the height, you won't get the strong heart, the fast-twitch muscle fibers, and the enhanced intelligence."

He was the doctor, so he must know best. His fingers flew over the tablet, tapping, tapping; creating a laundry list of desirable attributes. With every tap, the bottom line grew more and more terrifying.

"Five million!" gasped Kerry. "We can't possibly—"

Frowning, the doctor swept his hand along the tablet, and the total vanished from sight. "Don't worry about that!" He pointed at a much smaller figure, circled in black. "*This* is all you'll have to pay every month. We'll deduct it from your account. You won't even know it's gone."

Rob fidgeted. He would certainly notice if that amount was gone every month. It meant serious cuts to recreation and travel— and even to more casual purchases. They would be on a tight budget. . . probably for the rest of their lives.

"Too much?" the doctor asked, seeing Rob's expression. "No problem! We can reduce the monthly payment to *this*. It adds a few years to the payment, but Dayspring always does all it can to make our treatments affordable!"

Kerry turned her eyes away from the numbers, concentrating on the bright future they were creating for their little girl. What parent would not want the best for their child?

The doctor's manicured fingers tapped on inexorably: the bottom line swelled. Felix began asking probing questions about their assets, about collateral. He seemed to already know a great deal about their financial situation. Then he asked about their parents' assets, and how many siblings would share in any bequests after their deaths.

One thing had led to another. Now it seemed very natural to answer his questions. They gave their account information, and the doctor made a quick search of their credit ratings. Rob fidgeted again, wondering if he was being manipulated by the world's canniest used-car salesman.

"And of course," the doctor remarked, "recent legislation forbids bankruptcy proceedings involving gene-modification debt. It also mandates that in the event of your deaths, the debt devolves on the child herself, as the one profiting from the treatment. No problem with that, of course. Her future is assured, with all the advantages you're arranging for her!" Another blinding smile. "If nothing else, Dayspring International will take her on and find appropriate work for her until the debt is satisfied!"

Kerry's eyes fastened on the pictures of the pretty children, finding hope and validation there. *Their* child would not be limited to dead-end jobs; *their* child would not be shunted aside as an inferior Naturalborn.

They signed off on the tablet, were given an appointment for the first treatment, and staggered away under the weight of a note for a sixty-year loan, compounded semi-annually.

"I hope she likes having blue eyes," muttered Rob. "We'll be paying for them long enough. The odds are we won't live long enough to pay them off ourselves."

Kerry managed a tremulous smile. "They'll be no ordinary blue. They'll be Indigo Ocean eyes."

### 

### About the Author

Susan Nance Carhart has degrees in history and music, and enjoys doing things with them that would make her professors shudder. Mild-mannered bureaucrat by day and creator of fantastic worlds by night, she likes picking apart societal trends and projecting where they might lead. Truth really is stranger than fiction, but she tries to keep up.

Her stories have appeared in the anthologies *Horror, Humor, and Heroes,* volumes two and three, in *Buzzymag,* and in *365 Tomorrows.* She lives with her books, her harp, and her can-fix-anything husband in Naperville, Illinois.

*****~~~~~*****

# The Olinauts

by Adele Gardner

Marvelous Jones gripped the console as *The Spirit of St. Louise* shook. "Can't you stabilize this thing?"

"It's a delicate operation. Hold on, Marv."

A hollow clang. Marvelous straightened as Bert said quietly, "We're here."

They stepped out into darkness lit only by an arc light that kept buzzing on and flickering off. Marvelous shivered and hurried after Bert's long strides. The metal deck echoed in the open hold.

"Everything's so big here," Marvelous said as they hurried through another arch so wide it might have been a room. She staggered as the ship shuddered. Bert caught her.

"We've got to find the command room, and quickly."

Sparks shot along the ceiling. High on the wall, she spotted a plate hanging loose to reveal buttons, toggles, and thick, curved levers. A horn protruded near the top. "Do you suppose that's the speaking tube?"

"Good eye, Marv," Bert said, and hoisted her onto his shoulders. "The blue toggle, I think."

She pulled it and shouted, "Hello! We've come to help. It's Bert—he says you know him. Where are you?"

A trumpeting roared through the panel—so loud she lost her balance. Bert caught her and set her on the deck. "Hurry! Down the hall, left up the grassway, behind the savannah. Thank the Great Allomother you've come!"

They ran, the corridors blurring past, their vastness hard to fathom in the flickering light. Bert's checkered, old-school pilot's scarf streamed out behind; his giant bomber jacket flapped like wings. Marvelous wasn't sure if the tightness in her chest was lack of air, or the way

Bert jumped from one life-threatening situation to the next, never caring for the danger, whether it be alien warriors or ancient gods. He might not age, but how much longer before his heroism claimed his life? But she'd urged him to come as soon as she'd seen the holes in the ship that drifted across their scanner.

They raced through corridors vast as cathedrals, the flickering lights showing girders inside broken walls like mammoth bones. Walls swirled with painted blues, greens, and yellows, a giant landscape she could see only in patches. The long plains and scraggly trees carried an odd familiarity.

They ascended a grassy ramp. Bert stopped short. Marvelous caught herself on his outstretched arm. Before them, the fitful illumination showed a savannah mural, acacias scattered across broad grasslands, with hills rising into blue mist above. She swallowed. "It reminds me of Earth," she said.

"I think that's the idea," Bert said. With an arm extended above his head, he rapped the panel with his knuckles. "It's Bert—"

The mural slid aside. Blue light suffused a command room whose controls hung high above even Bert's head. With trees around the perimeter, grass and dirt covering the floor, and waterholes below the walls, at first Marvelous took them for part of the decor: large, leathery columns that swayed slowly as the ship listed. Great snakelike appendages weaved dexterously over the controls, flipping a toggle here, pulling a lever there.

She looked up to find a wise, wrinkled, gray face, the dark eyes luminous, the twin curving tusks yellowed with age. The trunk reached out and lightly draped Bert's shoulders.

"Bert. How lovely to meet again, here at the end. I am Oriendor, Matriarch-Captain," she rumbled. "We are grateful for a visit from an old friend, particularly one as old and wise as you, but there is no help for us."

118

Bert was virtually immortal; of hardy stock, he didn't look a day over thirty. His placidly ordinary face hid both his intelligence and the millennia he'd already traversed—most of it the hard way, he'd told Marvelous, though he'd recently equipped their jaunty ship with a time skate he'd forgotten he had. He'd repaired it, and they'd been testing it out, gleefully hopping from one lightyear to the next with the ease of skipping stones across a pond.

"Oh, there's always hope," Bert said, fondly patting the trunk. "And you're only as old as you feel. This is my friend, Marvelous Jones."

Marvelous said, "Please excuse me for being rude, but you're African elephants, aren't you? From Earth?"

Oriendor roared. "*Olifaunt*. You gave us that name. You who come from apes. We saw your kind rising up, lower animals, but cunning. Bert helped us long ago, when we might have doomed ourselves. His solutions were sensible, but afterward we realized what he represented. You apes were the future. You were too clever with those hands—and much too quick. We needed to claim the stars while we still had time." Oriendor raised her tusks with pride. "We left so many behind. They pledged never to betray our secret, never to reveal our intelligence to the apes, to buy us time. They all died in the end. But it was worth it, to have the stars, even for a little while."

"Oh, it's not over yet, Oriendor. Certainly not! Why, all you need are a few repairs!"

"More than that, Bert. We are the last—just two hundred of us. The final ship. In all your travels, surely you've seen the planet we're aiming for, Oranymede? Out of all the galaxy, it's the one spot we might reach that could provide a home for us now."

"I confess I haven't had time to visit. Rather a big universe, you know."

119

Marvelous craned her neck to see the screens above the workstations. Several showed an approaching spaceship. A nearby olinaut looped a trunk around her. She yelled, but quieted as she was lifted past a gentle eye and placed firmly on the elephant's back, where fur stood like sparse, fragile grass.

Oriendor said, "The humans have caught up with us at last. We all seek the same new Earths. And they are far more concerned with glory than the good of the herd. We have fled the battle hoping for one glimpse of Oranymede, our beautiful blue watering hole. But they will catch us."

Bert said, "Let me talk to them, Oriendor. Two reasoning species from the same homeworld—surely we can work something out."

After a murmured introduction, Marvelous stood on Eiora's head to view the archives. Thank goodness for the translator that Bert had inserted at the base of her skull; so much of the data was encoded in smells. Rumbles, snorts, and roars accompanied pictures of human spacecraft exploding, one after another—even though the earliest ships had displayed recognizable interplanetary peace signs.

"Bert," she said, keeping her voice low, struggling to stay calm. She felt suddenly as though they were trapped in an enemy camp.

At the tightness in her voice, Bert hurried over. Beside Eiora, Ophante lifted him onto her head. Taking off his jacket and rolling up his sleeves, he took control and sped through the archives. Human spaceships blew up outside olinaut worlds or in the common spacelanes.

Bert turned to Oriendor. "Matriarch, did you know about this?"

The great head drooped. The elephant rumbled, "Self-defense."

"You call this self-defense?"

"It was not our fault! They triggered our defensive devices!" Oriendor barked her anguish. "We knew the apes would follow us. We knew that violence was not the answer, but we did not wish to be destroyed. So we equipped our ships and planets with the power to throw any attacking force back upon the wielder—amplified ten times."

The systems warned them a ship approached. Eiora barked and rocked back. "Watch out!" Marvelous yelled, but all the olinauts were moving now, forming a circle around the matriarch.

"Matriarch, are your defenses still working?"

"Of course, Bert," Oriendor said.

"You can't destroy a ship full of sentient beings as your final act! Turn off your defensive grid!" Bert urged.

"We don't have enough power to turn it on again!" she roared. "They will destroy us!"

"We can talk to them, Oriendor. They're reasoning beings. You need to give them a sign of good faith."

Another olinaut brayed, "He speaks for the apes! Just look at him! Even though he met us first, he wears their form!"

Oriendor said, "He speaks for peace, as he's always done! The humans were destroying us without his help!" She wove her trunk through levers. "There. It is done!"

A human face stared back at them, as large as an olinaut on the giant screen. The dark, bearded man wore long braids and a zippered flight suit painted to look like leather. "What do you monsters want! Are you ready to die?"

Bert cut in. "Hello, Commander! I am talking to the Commander?" He offered a winning smile.

"Captain Brickson," the other grudgingly allowed.

"And I'm Bert. As you can see, we have turned off our offensive devices, and respectfully request that you do the same."

121

Brickson started. He leaned forward. "What are you, a traitor? No, you must be an alien; no human could be so stupid! Do you have any idea how many thousands of ships they've destroyed? How they blasted us when we tried to enter their atmosphere on peaceful missions?"

The olinauts ceased rumbling, ceased working, and bowed their heads.

Bert said, "Can't you see how sorry they are? That was all a misunderstanding—and it was a long time ago. Both sides have done untold damage—but neither of you started this war. They only want peace. Do you really want their deaths on your conscience?"

"I wouldn't mind," he drawled. He reached out an arm toward invisible controls.

"If you won't listen to me, listen to Marv! She's from Earth!"

"Marvelous Jones, at your service. He may not be human, but I am!"

"Really? You're a collaborator, then."

"Bert and I only came to help! Don't you recognize these people? They're *elephants*. We grew up together on Earth! They're from Africa, just like the first humans! Just like my ancestors! How can you possibly call them monsters?"

"Elephants? Elephants? That old story? Mythology. Legends. Monsters to scare children. They're about as believable as gryphons and basilisks. Elephants and unicorns! You tell that to all the humans they destroyed! If there ever were any elephants, they've been extinct for at least a thousand years!" Brickson leaned forward. "Now you listen to me. You're human, so I'll give you one last chance. You get off that ship—now. We'll take you on board—the scans confirm you're human—but I don't promise we won't convict you afterward."

Bert said, "Your admirals aren't around, so the decision rests with you. Kindly consider what you're doing. This ship contains the last olinauts. Surely you

The Olinauts

wouldn't want to be responsible for the ultimate destruction of a sentient species from your home planet!"

"They're all alone? So are we!" Brickson said savagely. The screen went dark.

"Get out of here!" Bert yelled. The olinauts scrambled at the controls as the ship rocked, under fire.

Marvelous watched the screens in horror as pieces of the ship spun away. The elephants roared their grief over one of the garden pods, where daughters tended food, a segment of the rambling walk where two males had been stargazing, and one of the nursery pods with three calves and five allomothers. The bulkheads held, but the ship strained with the loss of oxygen, rotational weight, and power.

"If we get out of this," Marvelous told herself, gritting her teeth, "I'm going to twist Bert's arm until he takes us back to pre-extinction Africa. We'll change things for the elephants before it's too late!"

The ship lurched. Marvelous slipped, but a trunk caught her. Eiora bellowed and swayed, her four feet as sturdy as trees. Their ship jumped—the screens flashed with stars—the black void burst into blue-white light— then the ship shuddered back into normal space. Below them, Oranymede shone blue, white, and green, a beautiful world that looked, even to Marvelous, an awful lot like home.

"At last!" Oriendor trumpeted. Her daughters raised their trunks and joined her. "After fighting for so long!" She confessed, "We had to get here first. We took the offensive, deliberately running into human ships. We used our defense grid like a weapon. The archives gave us the idea. They must have sacrificed a hundred ships before they discovered how to jump inside our shields. The best way to destroy us is a simple collision from inside the defensive grid, where our shields protect them as well. So many lives lost. What a nightmare our dream has become."

123

Bert muttered to himself as he shrugged his jacket back on and wandered the perimeter. "You jumped," he repeated.

"We must get to Oranymede—even if we die there—just to smell sweet grasses and drink fresh water under opens skies once more. This ship is a prison. We need grasslands, trees, space to roam. We need room for our males to challenge without endangering the herd."

Bert said, "What you need is a cooperative colony on equal footing. You'll only be safe if you learn to live with the humans, someplace where you can help each other until you're as close as sisters."

Marvelous called out, "Bert, Captain Brickson's going to be here any minute. He'll figure out where they've gone!"

"This ship won't survive another jump—not in this condition," Bert mused. "I could link it to *The Spirit of St. Louise*, but it won't stand a teleport. Oriendor! Are you willing to forgo hostilities with the humans?"

"They'll destroy us!"

"You'll have to trust me! Do I have your agreement?"

Rumbling filled the cavernous room as the matriarch consulted with her daughters. At last she trumpeted, "Yes! You have our consent!"

"Come on, Marv! Help me link the defensive grid to the time skate. Maybe, just maybe—"

Eiora and Ophante carried them back to the landing bay. Bert slipped into *The Spirit of St. Louise*, returning with cables. He stood on Ophante's head, her trunk steadying him as she reared so he could reach the highest panels. Marvelous followed instructions in the console room on *The Spirit of St. Louise*.

Back in the command center, Captain Brickson's ship arrived on screen—inside the defensive grid. Scanners showed their own hull shimmering with the time energy of the skate powering up. Marvelous had worked side by side with Bert to repair and augment *The Spirit*, and she didn't think it had the power to skip a ship this vast more than a few minutes away. They might dodge the first few blasts, but it wasn't a permanent solution.

Bert called, "Brickson! Listen to me! The olinauts are willing to negotiate, despite the fact that you've sheared off part of the nursery. Even though you've killed babies and mates, they still want peace!"

"I, Captain Brickson of the *Redoubtable*, claim this planet on behalf of the Archimedes Corporation—" Brickson intoned. His voice broke. "Don't you realize there is no more corporation! No other ships are coming to relieve us! These damned *elephants* have destroyed them all! And now, for them to claim our last refuge—"

"They're only here because you've driven them from their worlds. They have nowhere else to go. Surely you won't begrudge sharing one planet in this vast galaxy! And you're not alone. You're all children of Earth! The odds against two of you Earth species meeting out here are astronomical! Surely that must mean something!"

Brickson didn't answer. Marvelous held her breath. A flash of fire, across their bow—

The universe blinked. Brickson's ship vanished for a moment, leaving an unobstructed view of Oranymede. Marvelous drank in the beautiful blue-green sight, in case it was her last.

Their ship shuddered. The olinauts linked trunks.

Brickson's ship reappeared. The screens focused inward to show the *Redoubtable* attached to their ship in place of a vanished pod, the defensive grid holding them all together—with enough systems and resources between the two for one strong ship.

Bert said quietly into the intercom, "You'll need to work together, Brickson, if you want to reach that planet. *The Spirit of St. Louise* knows best. She's linked you all into one big ship now. But don't worry. Marvelous and I will stay long enough to help you."

"Please, Brickson," Marvelous added, her voice filled with pity. "There's too much beauty here to fight about."

"All right," he croaked. "All right!"

Marvelous smiled with relief. Bert grinned back at her. "I couldn't agree more."

### 

## About the Author

Adele Gardner has published stories in *Daily Science Fiction*, the Green Knight Press anthologies *Legends of the Pendragon* and *The Doom of Camelot*, *Penumbra*, *Challenging Destiny*, and *Scheherazade's Facade*. She's also had articles and poetry published in *Strange Horizons*, *Mythic Delirium*, and *The Magazine of Speculative Poetry*, among others. Two stories and a poem earned honorable mention in *The Year's Best Fantasy and Horror*. Much of this occurred under her previous byline, Lyn C. A. Gardner. Adele's story, "In the Garden," appeared in the Third Flatiron anthology, *Playing with Fire*.

*****~~~~~*****

# *Credits and Acknowledgments*

Cover Design - Keely Rew

Readers  - Andrew Cairns, Tom Parker, and Keely Rew

Thanks to Tracey A. Smith for her illustration for "Lost in the Mail" (ebook version only)

*****~~~~*****

**Discover other titles by Third Flatiron:**

(1) Over the Brink: Tales of Environmental Disaster

(2) A High Shrill Thump: War Stories

(3) Origins: Colliding Causalities

(4) Universe Horribilis

(5) Playing with Fire

(6) Lost Worlds, Retraced

(7) Redshifted: Martian Stories

# THIRD FLATIRON

www.ingramcontent.com/pod-product-compliance
Lightning Source LLC
Chambersburg PA
CBHW071318130626
46556CB00004B/1646